What We Both Know

What We Both Know

A Novel.

Fawn Parker

McClelland & Stewart

Trade paperback edition published 2022

McClelland & Stewart and colophon are registered trademarks
of Penguin Random House Canada Limited.

Published simultaneously in the United States of America.

Library and Archives Canada Cataloguing in Publication

Title: What we both know : a novel / Fawn Parker.
Names: Parker, Fawn, 1994- author.
Identifiers: Canadiana (print) 20210393556 | Canadiana (ebook) 20210393564 |
ISBN 9780771096730 (softcover) | ISBN 9780771096747 (EPUB)
Subjects: LCGFT: Novels.
Classification: LCC PS8631.A7535 W43 2022 | DDC C813/.6—dc23

Book design by Emma Dolan
Cover art: Emma Dolan
Cover design based on an image by Igor Ustynskyy/Moment/Getty Images
Typeset in Sabon MT Pro by M&S, Toronto
Printed in Canada

McClelland & Stewart,
a division of Penguin Random House Canada Limited,
a Penguin Random House Company

www.penguinrandomhouse.ca

1 2 3 4 5   26 25 24 23 22

Penguin
Random House
McCLELLAND & STEWART

For Elliot

What We Both Know

A note to the reader: this book includes depictions of animal death, child abuse (emotional and sexual), self-harm, and suicide.

1

THE EGG IS BOILED until firm. Rubbery outside and
chalky in the middle, a moment before it might form a dark
silvery ring around the yolk. The yolk will be removed, a
soft almost-sphere, the white discarded. The egg is boiled
on high heat for ten minutes, removed, placed on a paper
towel, cooled. A crack is made against the counter, the shell
chipped away into the damp paper towel which is bunched
then placed in the trash.

Baby is talking, talking.

I prepare the eggs, place one on a plate and slice
through with a butter knife. I'm doing it wrong; this one
is for myself. Should he take notice, he might interpret it
as some small act of protest. So I let him. Baby's egg has
been spread onto an over-toasted slice of sprouted bread.
He chews in a particular way . . . I can't watch. Mine, I'll
have on its own, maybe some plain cooked oats afterwards.

The kitchen is full of feeling. There's a lemon-scented
disc of wax that's been melted into an outlet-powered
warmer. The wax is sold in packages like small ice cube

trays, the cubes then melt into the top bowl-like portion of the apparatus. The lemon scent is dry, reminded me of yellow Pez candy when I first smelled it, now reminds me of itself and other moments taking a similar shape to this one. These types of things Baby doesn't care for, dismisses when asked, as if the object is naturally occurring—cobwebs, insects collected in the glass dishes of ceiling light fixtures, the like. Baby doesn't remember where the wax warmer is from, *who* it's from, as he wouldn't make such a purchase himself. His dismissal is permission for me to adopt the object and to use it when I please. I like the scent. I like the slow glisten as the yellow goes from soapy-dull to wet juice, then solidifies again. The eggs bump against one another and grow hard inside, the yellow wax softens.

I read that each time something is remembered it is changed. Each morning I remember how to make Baby's breakfast and surely I must do something differently. A wrong swipe of butter across bread, too much salt, the offensive addition of paprika. Baby recites his lines, doesn't know one egg from another.

My routine now is being streamlined into its most simple form. In the mornings I must do things right or there is a risk of getting thrown off. The housework comes first, then the real work, then the day. The day is what I'm talking about, the thing that can get thrown. I work quickly against the anxiety of losing the morning altogether. It's as if I expect I can exist outside of time.

The real work is the writing. Baby began outlining a new book, a memoir, just over a year ago, but in recent months he has been less and less able to put the ideas together.

The irony is not lost on me that the work is strictly from memory. This project, he told me, will finally cement his legacy. "Reveal the hand that holds the pen!" he'd said excitedly, most certainly after rehearsing it. I think really his characters were just getting too much attention. He has tasked me with crawling through his notebooks, rough notes he makes in his lucid moments day to day, and article clippings from reviews and interviews. Then I am to compile all of this information into a narrative, get it to the literary agent through his personal email, and nobody needs to know any more than that. It's true I would like to be working on something of my own, but I agreed out of excitement, having never before written for an audience. I've spent my life writing into thin air, my printer feeding it into my own hands, where it gets mailed to magazines, mailed back with a form rejection. I don't keep the work, usually, as if I can pretend that the failures don't exist. So far I've just had a piece in one of the magazines. The fiction one from the Prairies. But not much else to show.

I did have an idea for something longer. Oh, but it's silly. I'd been thinking about trying my hand at a long poem. The funny thing is, I've never even read one! Not all the way through. To commit so much time to a poem, to let it span a year, or even longer. I am so drawn to the slowness. The largeness. The way I could hide anything I wanted in there.

Anyway, I'm not too good at all. Baby has said before that Pauline "had the touch." He's not said anything about me to the contrary; it's just he hasn't said anything at all. I expect this project will propel me forward in my abilities, to mimic somebody great. And I've been considering how my name must affect things; it forces an association. Without it I may not have stood any chance at all. And with it, well they either expect so much or nothing at all. Really I am just another of his projects, and if I can help it not the one of least integrity.

But it's what I do, no? It's why I'm here. That and other reasons. And if I don't do the writing then there's not so much else to do, once the tidying up is done. At times I allow myself to do what comes naturally, for the moment at least. I bunch my duvet around my legs and watch the drapes dance with an afternoon breeze. In those moments I feel deserving of the slowness; for what I've *been through*. And what's that? Well for one thing I lost Pauline. But that was one year ago, and a day. The anniversary marked a conclusion to the chaos. Now we go on living again, without Pauline. Now every day, every season, is not the first without her.

Well, and there's Baby. Surely it must be difficult, my exposure to him and his decline, but at present I don't feel it. We do our small things. I take care of the errands, the meals. At the breakfast table he watches his tapes and recites the lines. The days aren't so bad.

So long as there's something to do in the evening, things are okay in a day. Dinner with a friend of Baby's later, and of course our usual routines. The washing-up, a crossword puzzle if we've time, and some of Baby's slow, repetitive exercises. The evening will eat itself up. So, the day should be good. After all, I chose this. I withdrew from my position at the university, broke my lease on the one-bedroom in Toronto's east end. It even had a little window seat, like I've always wanted. A place to *be*.

Now it's still early. I've had my coffee, not yet my tea. I drink Earl Grey because it reminds me of Pauline. She would always stand leaning against the kitchen counter, holding the mug in both hands. I do it too, sometimes, just to feel how it feels. I won't go on about that. Everyone is always missing someone. Besides at this point it has become my "thing" as much as it was hers, the tea. I barely think of Pauline sometimes. I don't do it how she did it either: black. I add some 2% and a pinch of white sugar. I am a bit softer of a person.

Baby is beginning to go more and more each day. Not so long ago he was in a place we called "on the edge." Myself and the doctor, that is. Back then I was just popping over for visits, finding excuses to check in on him. Then, last month, the doctor told me it was time. Now I live here. Now he is forgetting, moving things to new places they never would have gone before, not really answering my more direct questions ("Would you like to go now or wait and do something else first"—it was the *or*, I had deduced, that he didn't like; he would have to remember too much).

In the kitchen, he sits in front of his tablet, which is mounted in a desktop holster, and watches Charlie Rose ask him questions. On screen Baby laughs, answers first coyly and then at length. Yes, the duty of the writer is to insult one's friends and have them brag, "That's me!" He is handsome, dressed expensively.

"Yes," Baby says, pauses the video, mimics the coy expression. His mouth tenses, the corners turn down, and somehow he uses this shape to convey a certain suppressed joy. I turn away, give him the illusion of privacy. "The duty of the writer . . . ," he goes on.

My missing of Pauline—sorry, again about Pauline—has in a way prepared me for how I'll feel when Baby goes all the way. I've started to go through the motions of missing him already. For example, I've more or less stopped saying "dad" like I used to.

Yesterday I did some of my best work. I went through pages of Baby's notes, writing a scene from his childhood in which he is on a tour bus with his parents in Toronto, having to pee so badly that he considers jumping out of the vehicle, eventually reaching a rest stop and experiencing such bliss while urinating that he develops a habit of holding it in, as a teenager contracts a UTI, has to tell his doctor he is "addicted to peeing," ties this into a burgeoning fixation on genital release. I don't mind so much the more explicit writing as long as it concerns Baby's youth. So long as he's more or less sterile in present day. Long ago he taught me the difference between art and life, that there are special rules for each.

This morning I had a feeling of anxiety that while in my office, lost in my work, the rest of my life would get away from me. That I wouldn't think about the right things, would let my routines slip away. Mostly I was thinking about Pauline, how I worry I'll forget her even for a moment, though I try to see this fixation as a symptom of some inner artfulness and not something sad, clinical. Perhaps there is a more romantic edge to my grief. More than just that I had Pauline once, and now I don't.

Sometimes I feel that I died when Pauline died. Or, that I ended. When I consider life after her I do not feel that there was life then loss then life again, without her. I feel that there was life and then there was loss and now there is something . . . fast, light. Even the sadness feels contained in the life before, as if, yes, I would feel devastation were I still in the pre-life. But she is too far away now, and I am changed. I feel sad for those selves, but for the new self I have shifted into—I haven't decided yet.

Now, anything can happen. In the now, Pauline is dead. In the now, Baby is dying. In the now, I act in ways I do not recognize. I am old. I feel old in my permanent changedness. I feel that I am overstaying, pacing. And for that I hate Pauline, for she will never know the new life. She, the marker of change, singing the cue of the switch, the lipstick pop of then-then-now, then-now-now. And I sit at Baby's desk, and I cannot write because I am unskilled. I approach middle age. I have nothing to show for myself.

IN THE UPSTAIRS OFFICE there's a view of a field with a baseball diamond and a dirt track around the outside. I watched two children chase each other, their breath visible in the frigid air when they laughed and yelped. An orange ball rising in arcs between them, sometimes hitting the ground and being run after, was the only break in palette. The rest was grey, dark green, brown, including their fleece jackets and wool caps. Their father stood off to one side with a Thermos of something.

Here is the approximate layout of the house in bird's-eye view:

FIRST FLOOR

Living Room	Storage Closet	Coat Closet
Staircase	Baby's Office	Mud Room
Kitchen	Dining Room	Back Deck

SECOND FLOOR

My Office	Bathroom	My Room	Balcony
Baby's Room	Hallway	Pauline's Room	Balcony

Make sense?

I do wish I'd kept my own place. But desire must come second to some things, such as my situation with Baby. He has nobody else. Were I to treat this strictly as a job, arrive at nine and leave at five, then what? Sixteen hours he'd be in the house on his own.

The two floors of the house feel disconnected now that Baby so rarely goes upstairs. Often he will sleep on the leather couch in his office, in his clothes. It is like we are each in our own apartment, one on top of the other. If I am in my office and he is in his office it is like we are co-workers. It is becoming rarer that Baby will work unless I am downstairs, too. Mostly he comes slowly into a room once I am set up in there. Anyway, my work is his work and his work mine.

This morning I have more to do, setting the dining room table for when Catherine arrives, driving into town to fetch produce for dinner. The market closes at four, and I hope to get zucchini, button mushrooms, maybe some fresh tortellini if they have and make a sauce with plum tomatoes, basil, garlic, red wine.

2

LAST NIGHT I SAW my mother. I was surprised she'd agreed to come, more so that she followed through. Most of the group was my age, couples with young children, or artsy-looking girls in smock dresses. Most of them were Pauline's friends from university, or friends of friends. What I noticed was how her ex-boyfriend was not there, though he had phoned me to personally RSVP.

In a circle around the dining table we told stories about Pauline. Some didn't sound like Pauline at all. *That's not right*, I wanted to say. *Pauline wouldn't do that*. Baby laughed when we laughed, nodded; we skipped him when it came to his turn. He didn't realize, surely. He nodded again, looked attentively at the woman to his left. I kept an eye on him, thinking somehow that if I watched closely enough, I could prevent him from acting out. The secrecy of his condition felt at times like a heavy container of water I carried with me, always about to spill.

My mother rocked in her chair and held her amethyst necklace.

The name must have finally resonated with him because Baby interrupted the woman who was speaking, exclaiming, "Pauline!" He looked around the table. "When will Pauline arrive? We've been waiting all evening!" He looked as if he might punish her, should she arrive, which, of course, she wouldn't.

No answer would satisfy him. I tried to calm him, but when he is like that, I am his enemy. He pulled his arm out of my grip. A server came to check on us, then returned to ask if we could remove Baby from the restaurant, his episode was disturbing other diners. In getting up from his seat, Baby's knees bumped the table, knocked over a handful of glasses, some into the laps of Pauline's friends.

"Why is she shutting me out?" he asked us, each of us, over and over. For a moment I wondered if he meant my mother.

Eventually I shepherded him out. I looked into the anxious faces around the table, tried silently to communicate something between an apology and a plea for help.

Baby sat in the passenger seat while I said goodbye to my mother. I'd wanted them to have a moment together, for her to find something in him that nobody else could see. She'd watched him from across the table. A spectacle, none of her business.

"Don't you let him have you." She shook her cigarette at me. She'd looked glamorous, old. As if the more she lost her children the more she regained herself. Besides, I say *lost*, but it's her disinterest that divides us, her and me. This was the first she'd so much as mentioned Baby all evening. Her train was early the next morning, which left no time for another meeting. I searched for something significant to say, she squeezed my shoulder, and I got into the Jeep to take Baby home. In my rear-view mirror I saw her watching just as at dinner. None of her business.

I dress quickly and facing away from the mirror. My body on certain days seems too much to bear. My mother said once on her birthday, clutching at her head, "But I still feel twenty-five!" She was sixty-five and making a joke, but the joke came out sounding like despair. I do not feel this way, but I don't know what to make of my age either. My clothes are modest, in dark and earthy colours. I disguise the curve of my lower half, that way it looks like it must belong to somebody else.

Sometimes I wonder if Baby can see me.

I must set him up with enough things to do while I am out of the house. At present he is still doing his great important work of watching the old interviews, of consuming himself once more. Each morning he wakes up empty, must drink himself down. Then a little life shines through him, like the pink of a flamingo. It's only due to the fish they eat, you know.

To his right he has a stack of books: some his own, some others he likes to flip through. To his left, an e-reader loaded with more of his own, and more of others'. I've laid everything out on the waxy kitchen tablecloth. Its red check is tacky and out of place among the other, noble furniture in the house. It's just he's liable to spill. He runs his hands over it uneasily when he's thinking, as if he might be able to place the thought if he could just feel the warmth of the wood of the table. I always think of his mind as fading away, when perhaps really it's that it's buried under layers?

Another pot of coffee brewing, and there are leftovers in the fridge from the restaurant last night. Limp asparagus and some mushroom ravioli in cream sauce. I'll zap it before I go and leave it on the counter for Baby. He doesn't have much of an appetite midday. We have our breakfast and most days it's a fight to get anything into him before dinner. Left on his own he'd be content with a dinner roll and a glass of beer.

"Okay?" I say. If I leave now there will still be good produce at the market. By noon the fresh herbs are all but gone.

He puts his finger on a word in one of the books. "Market?"

I nod. "Do you want to come?"

"No," he says, into the book. "Well, no, I don't know."

"Just a couple things. We could have samosas and hot chocolate at the indoor tables." Surely it would be easier to leave him, but he wants to go fewer and fewer places. I feel it's my obligation to press him.

"No," he says. He shakes his head. "No."

He closes his book with a certain punctuation. There is turbulence running across his face. Then, rearranges his stack, opens another one, and twirls one finger in the air like he's conducting. "Ah," he says. "Yes."

At the restaurant last night, Pauline's friend Laurel sat with her baby on her knee and her arm across the baby's chest and the baby periodically reached out her hands at something, straining against her mother's arm. When we raised our glasses in cheers, the baby was not held back by the arm for a moment or two, and she sat still with her back against her mother's body. Once or twice Laurel chewed small bits of food and then placed them in her baby's mouth. I kept sneaking glances in awe, wondering when a mother and child separate into two people. I watched my own mother leave most of her plate, asked her if she wanted to try some of my meal. She declined.

THE MARKET IS ALIVE with movement in all directions. A woman with her hair pulled back and a canvas bag over her shoulder leans forward over a counter, points at a cut of meat. A gangly college student shouts coffee orders to a hunched older man who dries metal parts on his apron by an espresso machine. I see a couple of people I've known since childhood, with their families, and I act as if I haven't. I order an Earl Grey latte and take it to the indoor seating area where I sit at a bar along the back market wall, two seats down from a well-groomed baker sipping a double espresso. Most weekends I buy a loaf of sourdough from him or from his sister, and sometimes these long twisted breadsticks with rosemary. Though their family are friends of my parents, I assume that they do not remember me.

"When do you eat a food like this?" Baby asked the first time I brought home the breadsticks. "It's not a meal, not a breakfast, not a dessert. In twenty-four hours it's hard as a rock." Once in a while I'll bring some home just to needle him. We eat them alongside hard cheeses, broken pieces of dark chocolate, prosciutto and salami.

The baker is looking at me, I can tell, but when I turn he turns too. I wonder if I am multiple people to him; if he recognizes me but isn't sure I'm not someone else. I return to the stands every weekend, pick up more or less the same items, but I've made no move to develop a rapport. It's not that I don't want to. I always feel I'm watching the market like a film, alone and unable to affect anything, but playing a small, silent role. A half-participant.

I could turn to the baker and say something. We could walk arm in arm through the market, filling my cloth bags with fresh produce and little containers of whipped honey and long slender beeswax candles, in pairs of two connected at the wick. I could offer him one, ask if he could give me a ride home and on the way stop at his house to clip the candles apart, place one on his dining room table where I would lay down and offer myself. I feel sick at the thought. Lately when I have a sexual thought my breasts ache—not in desire but in panic. I dress carefully, rarely look at them. Sometimes, all of a sudden, my nipples will harden. Each time it makes me uneasy, like trying on a piece of clothing that is too young for me.

"London fog?"

I am shaken from thought. "What?" I say to the baker.

"I can smell it." He smiles.

Somehow I feel molested. What else can he smell?

I smile. "Any sourdough left today?" I ask. I try to communicate to him that he represents bread to me. That's it.

CATHERINE IS READING A passage to us from her journal at the dining room table. The dinner dishes are in front of us, streaked with red sauce and dry basil. My head is elsewhere. I'm wanting to get drunk. No one has reached for a second round from the bottle, so I don't either. It's when I'm drinking that things fall into place around me. A woman grins childishly at me in the mirror. Whatever it is I think I am otherwise falls away, a small death. I haven't been out in a little while. Not since I left the city. In my memory, I am unable to separate the city from my drunkenness. What else did I do there? I went to work, I waited out the weeks, the weekends fell through my hands like water. Each Friday, Saturday evening felt like my last, pulling through piles of once-worn clothes, looking for something that might make me outgoing.

Pauline used to say I romanticize negative things. "It's your gift and your curse," she said. "You love to feel bad." Recently I've slowed down. Well, I am slowing. I take things easy. Try not to make anything into something more than it is.

Baby is fading. He has been lulled by the sound of Catherine's voice, indifferent to what she's reading. I hear anything about a woman and I connect it to Pauline, see things that aren't there. This makes me tense, and I drain my glass to appear unaffected. Catherine goes on, doesn't seem to consider whether or not we're following. Her voice is hoarse from our earlier laughter, and the dry wine. I keep returning to her mouth, as if I might learn something about how to speak. Always I am searching for ways to conceal myself, to become more like anybody else. Her lips are thin and pale, with small delicate lines in the surrounding skin. She reads how she was not expressive with her mother. Things went unsaid.

With Pauline, the problem is no one person was enough. We could pass her off, myself, her ex-boyfriend, her roommate, one at a time, but she always felt the absence of the others. That is, when she wanted us. At other times she spent long stretches alone, gave few details of her whereabouts. When she needed us, she needed us. She would call in the middle of the night, sobbing, then hang up, deny it in the morning. Plus we all had problems ourselves. I felt I couldn't care for her and care for myself, not enough at least. It was her leaving that made me stop caring so much for myself. If she could meet the person I am after losing her, things might go differently.

Catherine reads a line about losing a book in the lake, having dropped it off the side of a dock.

"What was the book?" Baby says, suddenly alert again. "Pauline?"

"I don't remember," says Catherine.

Baby sometimes will slip and call Catherine "Pauline." He doesn't mean to, but he has begun to merge them. It startles me each time, as if he is casting a spell. A curse. I can't lose one more. Plus, this is his way of distancing himself. He has given up on the notion of having fathered Pauline, for fathering would include too much failure. Just think of what has come of it.

Catherine goes on about her mother, how she connects her mother to her female friendships, how she feels she is a mother to all women. The death of her own mother opened a vast empty space for her to fill. Plus it signalled the end of the transition from youth. Now, at fifty-six, she is truly, finally, a woman. She says this as if with an edge

of scolding, perhaps at least condescension. I have my
mother. I have my eggs. It must frustrate her to see that I
am not happy. This causes me to feel naked, that she seems
to know about my dissatisfaction. She knew me in childhood; we never connected.

I saw a therapist, after Pauline. "Is it fair to say you were
depressed as a child?" they asked.

Now Catherine and her mother walking by the canal in
the wind, in Montreal. They are in long jackets, I imagine.
The unpleasant weather romanticizes things, gives them a
reason to be quiet. Really it was summer, I'm beginning
to realize as she reads on. There is a sun slowly setting.
Catherine reads, "We searched for more to say."

I look to Baby and see he is ready to sleep.

Catherine and I move to the front porch to drink the
rest of the bottle of wine. She has borrowed a blanket and
an oat-coloured lotion I bought at the market in town,
rubs it into her hands and over her knuckles. She has a
peculiar way of doing it; she'll put some in her palm and
rub her other hand's fist into the cream, back and forth.
It's a wide shallow tub, and she scoops out the cream with
three fingers. She feels at home in our house; I can see in
the way she moves through it, the way she comes in without knocking.

My mother still brings her up on occasion, when she
really gets into it about Baby. It's always, "That tramp!"
I didn't see Catherine the first few times she came to the
house. I was seven, maybe eight, hiding upstairs in my
bedroom. I heard three voices, my mother's the most infre-
quently. From the sounds of it my mother stayed downstairs

in the living room. Baby brought Catherine up to his office and when she was leaving they talked about a number, I saw, crouched at the top of the staircase, that he took money out of his wallet and gave it to her. That first night my mother slept in my bedroom with me, silently. Then she always slept in my room when Catherine had been to visit, then she slept in my room a lot. How sick I had felt when I'd first learned about the things I could do with just myself, with my body, and how I'd had to do them so secretly and quietly in bed beside my mother. Afterwards I would say a prayer that I might die in my sleep, as punishment for being so sick.

Catherine hums, sips her wine.

"Are you cold?" I ask her.

She moves her head back then forth. Her mouth is pressed upward at the corners.

"I'm sorry he wasn't all there tonight."

"Oh," says Catherine. "He means well."

I have a sense of urgency about wanting to enjoy the evening. The small amount of remaining light and the chill creeping under our wool blankets. There's not too much left.

"I've always read him my journals," she says. I realize I'd not answered her earlier, perhaps suggesting I disagree. "I'm a writer, too, in that way," she smiles.

Again I search for something, anything, to say.

Catherine goes inside and retrieves little butterfly-looking curled cinnamon cookies from a tin. Something nags at me. Something has changed, and maybe it's that she wants to leave, or unrelated to me she wants to be

alone, to go to sleep. Was I meant to say something, perhaps reassure her, about her mother? Do something some
specific way, accept her into me in a way I unknowingly
resist? Really, I would. I can't decipher which of us is
resisting. There is no reason we cannot be something. It's
just I can't be with her without feeling my mother must
somehow be aware.

Then it is gone. Now, as a slackness returns to her
cheeks (a dimple disappears), I have to wonder if there
ever was a change. She bites into a cookie with one hand
cupped under her chin to catch the crumbs, sprinkles them
into the grass beneath like seedlings.

3

EARLY MORNING AND OUT the window the landscape is like a postcard. I am at the small wooden desk in my office with a single drawer, packed full of scraps and lists and receipts. My back aches in the kitchen chair, but I use the pain as a timestamp signifying I've been here long enough to've gotten some good work done. Mindlessly I sort through the papers in my desk drawer searching for something of meaning.

Wind whistles through small undetectable holes in the window frame. I've spent hours trying unsuccessfully to locate and fill them in, to prevent the small ladybug-looking beetles—they're not ladybugs, Baby insists—from crawling inside to escape the freezing temperatures. I'll admit I will smack one of them with a heavy hardcover every now and again. So many of them I spare, and bask in my own good-will. It is when I find them crawling in shiny hair-legged networks on the windowsill that I abandon my altruism. You may imagine then that the whistling wind is only a reminder of the bugs' easy access.

I become distracted so easily by the sounds of the house. It winds itself up in the morning, vibrates with light and life, and then slowly shrinks back into itself at night, groaning as it relaxes in the dark. From in here, I can't tell which sounds are the house and which are coming from Baby. Though his bedroom is the closest room to my office, we are separated by the stairwell, and I am given the illusion of remoteness. Once or twice I think I've heard the first stirs of his waking. Any time there is complete silence I am prevented from working. I have to wonder if he is up to something—if any moment disaster will strike.

Really I may be overly concerned with Baby's routines. There was only once when he got himself into trouble, trying to remove the screen from the kitchen window so he could water the seeds I'd planted. Otherwise it's with no small amount of trouble I try to discern where his need ends and my anxiety begins. Besides, now the window planters are wooden troughs of snow.

So, the memoir:

I must keep things as true as possible. I mustn't embellish as a narrator, as I am not the narrator. It is important that I leave no trace of myself. For this reason the work has been coming out cold and mechanical. I've felt unable to insert myself into the room—it's just, I really wasn't there.

It's all coming so slowly. If I cleaned it up I might have a chapter or so, at best. I don't know how he does it. I used to watch him during my childhood, the way he

could sit at his desk for hours and it would come right
out of him. Perhaps he is right that I really just don't have
the touch.

I try to break it down into a system, as if made up of
small individual parts, or of numbers. Each word must go
somewhere, and then it all must break even. A number of
words per day for a number of days. If I am to discover
the formula—neutral and objective—the memoir will be
perfect. Or it will go unnoticed altogether . . .

Ah, he is up.

He goes downstairs to dress in his office.

Soon we begin again. The eggs, bouncing in their shells
in their bath of boiling water. The toast jumps up when the
toaster's timer dings. There is a full-bodied kitchen smell
filling the downstairs.

Baby takes his place at the kitchen table, places his
hands flat on the tablecloth. We exchange a sheepish smile,
as if we still are new to this old, tired routine.

I am distracted by the challenges of the chapter I'd been
working on upstairs. It's an early portion, about mine and
Pauline's childhood. Baby taking a break between promotional tours, becoming increasingly agitated by the static
environment of the domestic household. Causing different
types of trouble just to punctuate the passage of time—
bringing women into the house, drinking late into the
night, spoiling one or both of us so that my mother would
be made the enemy. No matter the scene, if it takes place
in the house, I can't help but see things from the perspective of Pauline's doorway. When I try to write downstairs,

in the opposite corner of the house, the details are all obscured by the staircase. I try and try to be a writer but instead I am a sister.

"Nice day out," says Baby.

"Like a postcard."

I crack an egg against the countertop.

4

WE ARE TO BE at the literary agency for noon, when Baby has a meeting with Mark Richman, his agent of forty-five years. While he's there I will pick up Baby's prescriptions, and use the Xerox machines at the post office to scan some of his documents and mail them off to the government office in Ottawa. The morning has been difficult. See, I'd planned to get some work done prior to the drive into Toronto, but Baby was having difficulties with his wardrobe. Just something simple and nice, I'd told him. Each time I left him to get dressed I would return to find him on the edge of the bed, watching the closet like a television. Really he wanted things to be chosen for him. I was being difficult, too. I resent when I know what he wants. At the suggestion of a wine-red button-down we'd gotten on our way.

I am hungover just a little bit, in a way I find almost pleasant. Baby is in the back seat of the Jeep with a paperback copy of his 1979 novella *Nervous Habits*. The book was released before he became more widely recognized as a short story writer, and it went out of print before I was born. We were able to track down a used copy on Amazon through a bookseller in Syracuse, New York, but the book accidentally went to my mother's address in Kingston due to the shared account I years ago set up for them. She saw this as some sort of sadistic act upon receiving the book, and it took some amount of convincing for her to agree to package it back up and ship it to us at the house. "What a happy, happy accident," she barked over the phone.

Baby has angled himself against one of the back doors, legs across the back seat, and has the book in one hand, half of it folded around its spine, and is speaking quietly at the page.

"No, said Richard, it's a matter of scale, he had the thick unselfconscious lenses of an academic, gentle hands, something unattractive about their neatness to Marcia, made her too aware of her own, plus she wasn't speaking, probably not paying attention, the sharp profile of her face angled toward the train window, catching a yellow gleam."

"Okay," I say, and turn off the car.

Baby dog-ears his page, folds the book in his lap, sorts out his posture. "No," he says, "said Richard. It's a matter of scale."

I've had to park a few blocks away from the building, which faces right onto Bloor Street. The agency is located on the ninth floor of a skyscraper that also houses a number of psychotherapy offices, a law firm, and a restaurant and café on the ground floor. This building is a different one than where the agency had been in my childhood. At least, I think so. I recall being driven somewhere in the northern part of the city, to a home office of some sort, being served hot chocolate by a shiny-haired woman with big chunky rings on her fingers and a long flowered dress. Mark and Baby had gone off to some other part of the house while I got to sit at the big wraparound desk in the office and talk to the shiny-haired woman about how when I grew up I'd like to be a writer like my dad.

"Ready?" I say. I clap my hands down over the wheel in a way that reminds me of my mother.

"Home at last," he says. At this I feel a pressure behind my eyes.

I go around to the back and open Baby's door for him. "We've arrived at Mark Richman's office," I say. "You have a meeting about your new book."

"Ah," he says. "Yes."

"Do you remember Mark Richman?"

He fusses with his jacket, shoves the novella into an inner pocket. "Mark Richman!" He comes alive, looks to the front seat as if to find Mark there. "He wants to end me. To ruin my career."

"I don't think he'd do a thing like that."

"He wants to shelve me in romance! He wants me in book clubs!"

"Why don't we go talk to him and see?"

"I won't talk to that prick," he says. "That prick," he says again, takes his book back out of his pocket and returns to reading.

The hangover has turned on me; I have an unusual short-age of patience for him. So, I leave him, and go alone into the building and take the elevator up to the literary agency.

AS A YOUNG WRITER in the late sixties, Baby had been part of a collective of English grad students (although he himself was in the third year of his undergraduate degree at this time) who called themselves the Arthurs—initially Arthur's Knights of the Round Table—and ran a small zine out of the university's magazine office. The zine was released independently from the official university maga-zine but used the majority of its resources to print on fairly high-quality paper and access the mailing list database to reach out to other Canadian university publications, etc. The Arthurs handed out copies on Bloor Street and were notorious for hassling passersby, sometimes pressing cop-ies of the zine into chests, shouting, "If poetry is a dying art . . . prove it!" and tearing up copies and handing them out in piles of shreds. There is a framed photograph of Baby in a white T-shirt with *DON'T READ THIS!!!* written in black permanent marker across the chest, holding a stack of zines and looking wild-eyed at the camera, wearing business slacks cut at the knee and a backwards cap in mid-February sleet.

But one of Mark Richman's first moves when he signed Baby on was telling him he'd better "cut the damn stunt shit," and he'd had to put some distance between himself and the other Arthurs. This understandably was met with some backlash, and the very next issue of the zine— titled, by the way, *Sword & Stone*—was the "Beheading Issue," featuring a caricature of Baby on its cover, with the distorted likeness of his head bleeding and resting upside down at his feet.

Even today the rest of the Arthurs continue to publish locally and often collaboratively with one another. They don't get much recognition outside of the province, but locally they are perhaps the biggest names in the independent scene. Sort of like grandfather figures to young aspiring experimental writers. Or, so, that's how it's been explained to me. I don't know if now they've perhaps been cast out by the new literary generation. The whole lot of them, Baby included, are hard-headed and closed to change. They dress in the same vests and corduroys as in old photographs from their university days, keep thick moustaches and bowl-ish haircuts, and worship the classics. Ask any one of them and I bet they couldn't tell you the name of a living Canadian writer with a major-press publication.

Baby has often bitterly used the phrase "keeping one's seat at the round table" to suggest stagnation and a lack of commercial success. Baby encouraged me to make what he called "career moves." "Keep an eye on the big picture." I don't think he realized the smallness of my life as it stands. I move from room to room; I drive to the grocery store, the post office; I see Catherine, sometimes; and I miss Pauline. My job is I take care of Baby and he pays me. If he didn't pay me now it would be money I'd get through an inheritance. So in a way he's charging me, he likes to say. Before I moved in I didn't have much more going on. I kept to myself, worked in administration in the creative writing department. I got the position because of Baby, because he'd taught in the creative writing program. When it comes down to it I've never gotten an honest job, not anything other than picking up plates in a bar.

Mark Richman now, as compared to photographs of him and Baby pinned to the walls in Baby's office, appears fragile. But then, so does Baby. Mark mutters to himself while he makes me a coffee, picks through the top drawer of one of his filing cabinets. I've had to lie about Baby's absence and tell Mark that it is due to his current writing schedule that he is unable to make it into the city until a contract needs signing. I have no way of knowing whether this is usual behaviour in the dynamic between the men, whether this is allowed in publishing, even, but Mark does not push me for answers.

The office is lined on two walls with bookshelves, all full of leathery hardcovers. On the third wall, a small square window and a brass cart with an espresso maker and small tins and boxes of tea and coffee. A photograph of himself accepting some accolade. He looks handsome, and big, like a rugby player.

"So," he says. He sets a mug down in front of me, another one in front of his chair and then sits down. "What's the project?"

"It's a memoir."

"Okay," he says, but it sounds like a question.

I try to recall Baby's phrasing, when he's talked about it. It's always been "the memoir." That always seems grand enough, to him.

I take a sip of coffee and the heat surprises me, scalds my tongue.

"Do you take anything?"

My focus is on pretending not to have felt the pain. "What?"

"Your coffee. Do you take anything?"

"Oh, no. It's fine."

"It's fine now that you've had a sip? Because to ask for milk or sugar would imply that it's no good? Had I asked before you had some, would you have asked for something?"

"I'm not sure," I say.

"Alone in my office, you've just heard I've passed away, you go to the coffee cart for something to do, no, it's not a heartless act, you're in shock. You make a coffee. Milk? Sugar?"

"It's good," I say.

His arms are mid-air; he's engaged in the energy of the scenario. He deflates.

"So the memoir," he says, and his tone has changed. I fear he has realized I have nothing of value to tell him. "What's the angle?" He seems disappointed that I won't play with him. The truth is I don't know how. Baby would know. I on the other hand wasn't born with the gift of ease.

"It's going to tell it all," I say. "Things he's never told."

"What kinds of secrets is he keeping from me?"

"It's going to break down all of the ways he has wronged everyone in his life."

"Now there's a Baby Davidson idea," he says. "Called, ah, *A Table Bedecked in Cards*." He laughs.

"Yes," I say. "Something like that." I realize too late I'd been meant to laugh.

There is a silence.

"When can I have it?" he says.

"Oh," I say, "um."

"Is he far in? Is there a draft? A skeleton?"

"A skeleton for sure."

"I'll draft a letter. I'll need a synopsis, and then I'll need some pages."

"Okay," I say. "I'll tell him."

Somehow I'd let myself believe I'd get away with there being no book. I realize I've romanticized the industry to the point of seeing it as entirely abstract. All along I've thought Baby worked only in ideas. I never gave him the credit of logging long hours on the page. I do have some pages. But am I really going to send them to Mark? *Those* pages?

"Tell him to shoot off a few chapters to my email when they're ready. And to call me. I haven't heard a thing for months. He doesn't have to send you in and waste your time. You're busy"—he waves his hands—"I'm busy. Okay, good. Good?"

"Good." I nod. A few chapters when they're ready. My anxiety about the writing is somehow reversed. How long is this all going to take? By the time they've found a publisher Baby won't recognize his own name on the cover. Then, how do I suppose they'll believe he wrote the thing?

His readers are such hungry animals. University students write papers on the minutiae in novels he published decades ago. Sure, I can posture, but for how many pages can I pretend to be Baby before I slip and reveal my own voice?

"Actually," I say. "How about I get him to send the whole thing?"

"It's done?"

"Well. Soon it will be."

"Soon." He sits back, satisfied. As if this is how he wanted things to go.

IT'S A SHORT WALK to the pharmacy, so I circle back to the car so I can check to make sure Baby is still okay. Through the windshield I can see a silhouette in the back seat, upright, things seemingly in order.

Side by side on Bloor Street are two buildings: a family-owned pharmacy and a Canada Post office where Baby rents a PO box. At home the mail is collected in boxes grouped together at the end of the road, and ours will from time to time receive mail addressed to Pauline, my mother, or myself. Since Pauline, he has avoided the local box. Slowly he has begun to have all of his mail addressed to the PO, business or not.

Along the walls of the pharmacy are shelves and shelves of over-the-counter products. I leave a prescription for donepezil with the woman behind the counter, take a pamphlet on memory loss with my back turned to her in case she remembers me, tells someone. The owner is a family friend, which is what makes Baby believe it is the only place that won't give him the wrong stuff, cut it with something

lethal or, worse, give him something weaker than necessary.
To be honest I don't know anymore what's in the cocktail
of pills he takes; the names all blend together, and I just
mark small Xs on a paper schedule in the kitchen. The less
I know, the less I think about his death. The memory loss
I'm comfortable with; the physical death makes my skin
crawl. Anyway, I'm grateful for the stranger working today,
meaning I don't have to stay and chat. Instead I slip out
and go next door to the post office.

In one of Baby's old briefcases I've got folders of documents confirming his birth, his parents' names, the schools
he attended from the ages of four until dropping out at
fifteen, only to miraculously be accepted into university
at eighteen. I am to scan each one and staple all of them
together, mail them to a government office along with a
completed form requesting information on the adoption
that took place in July of 1952, when Baby was brought
into the Greene family. We have gone through this process
twice now, each time being notified six weeks later that
there was information or documentation missing. I worry
that this too is something that may happen too slowly. By
the time things are complete Baby may have forgotten this
part of himself.

The adoption was closed, meaning nothing could be
legally provided by the adoption agency or the city, but due
to a call last winter notifying him of the death of his biological mother, he now was able to file a request for some
of her records. In addition, he subscribed to an ancestry
site to try to find cousins, siblings, anyone. The problem
was there was no father. Well—on Baby's birth certificate

(and this is where "Baby" originated: in the adoption he was listed as Baby Davidson, just as others were listed as Baby Other-Surname; he was later renamed Marcus Greene, but he started using his pre-adoptive name pseud-onymously as advised by Mark Richman to distinguish himself from his notorious Arthurs personality) the man listed as the father is also Baby's mother's father, meaning, well, there are a few possibilities. One of them being that the father was simply absent and so the form had to be filled in by someone.

In the PO box there is a letter from a DNA testing com-pany, one from an ancestry website, and some royalty cheques, all of which I stuff inside of the briefcase.

When I return to the pharmacy to pick up the pinched little paper bags of prescriptions, the owner is behind the counter. The woman from before is nowhere to be seen, and I wonder if she's told the pharmacist I was in earlier looking at the pamphlets.

"Hillary!" he calls. A bell jingles behind me as the door closes. He has a plastic basket in front of him with two white paper bags inside of it. He asks me how my father is. I consider telling the same story as I told to Mark, about the hard work. Instead I tell the pharmacist that the city stresses him out, that he's settling back into the quiet of small town life. That he's moved back into the house I grew up in not because my mother finally gave it up but because it had been the plan all along. Well, I don't tell him that part.

"You know what he used to say to me," says the phar-macist.

"What's that," I say.

"He'd come in here and he'd say, 'Doc Laughlin, what's the difference between you and me?' And, you know, he'd've told me last time, and I'd go, 'Well,' I'd say, 'what is it, Mr. Greene?' And he'd go, he'd say, 'You have more patients!'"

With this he offers me the prescriptions, laughing.

"Only one who ever called me doc," he says.

I FEEL THE MEMORY loss pamphlet against my hip, or I imagine I do, when I get back into the car. I play out scenarios in which Baby finds it and something irreparable happens between us. Or worse, he's interested.

In the fourth grade it was suggested to my parents that I should be put in therapy. Both me and Pauline, actually, though if I remember correctly the conversations happened at different times, for different reasons—mine being due to a general sort of lackadaisical attitude and inability to properly assimilate with other students. That is to say I roamed the school field alone, participated in class only when addressed directly, stood still and white-faced in the gymnasium during any team-based game. At this suggestion, Baby, and in turn my mother, as she often in my upbringing sided with my father fervently, took immense offence to this attack on the family unit and our propensity for "us-against-them" behaviour, which, they insisted, signalled high intelligence and independent, creative thought. Plus my grades were the highest in my year, though I should note that my mother wrote all of my assignments for me, acting as if I was a pest for offering input.

"Mail from the ancestry site," I say. He is consumed by his book and doesn't respond. I keep the DNA testing results a secret for now, wanting to wait until I screen them for anything that might cause a fuss.

When I get onto Highway 401 he perks up and angles himself again toward the backseat window, forgetting the book. He becomes consumed by the traffic. If he watches close enough, there can't be an accident. Sometimes a car on the other side of the highway divide will drive in our direction in a particular way that catches Baby's eye and he'll press his hands and his forehead to the window and shout, "Slow down, slow down, slow down." When I exit the highway I feel him relax. Evening comes quickly, as if we've pulled the day shut with the Jeep, rumbling down Concession Road 7. On the more heavily-bushed side roads there are no lamps, putting us in complete darkness outside of the circle of our headlights when there are no other drivers on the road. When there is an oncoming vehicle, which is rare, especially on weekday evenings after the work rush, there's a sense of being watched.

When we return to darkness, my eyes are fuzzy and I can no longer feel the edge of the road. Baby taught me to watch the reflection of lights on the telephone wires for oncoming traffic. A trick he learned while driving delivery trucks in between his bachelor's and master's degrees. He delivered stacks of plastic bins, full of one hundred books each, to wholesalers and dollar stores in the towns surrounding Orillia, where he lived in a bachelor apartment in a building owned by his father. He felt a unique sort of peacefulness while driving the books to the stores and the empty bins back to the warehouse unmatched by any other activity, including reading and writing, which both made up his forty-plus-year career. He considered withdrawing from his master's program on multiple occasions to keep up the driving, maybe never do anything else, but his back started to get to him, and he got scouted by an agent (Mark Richman, that is) who'd been keeping an eye on the writing program at the university. When Baby was a student there wasn't such a thing as a bachelor of creative writing, so the novelists entered the professional writing and English literature programs, where they would get jobs editing the school lit mag, often printing their own work and leaving submissions unopened on the office shelves. Mark found out Baby had been submitting manuscripts to small local publishers and made him send them letters informing them that the work was no longer available, that they shouldn't read it, and then he, the agent, went to the big conglomerate publisher and told them he had something they needed to take a look at right away. This was what would later be titled *V Formation*.

He advised too that Baby stop teaching.

"The academy is a great set of training wheels," he'd said. "But you're riding on your own now."

WHEN I PULL IN Baby is back in his book. He doesn't mind the side roads, trusts me to get him to the end of the driveway. He likes to sit a minute and relax before going into the house. I heard somewhere that entering a doorway refreshes the mind, explains why often when a person goes into a room to do something or retrieve something they immediately forget their reason for being there, and I mistakenly told this to Baby, instilling in him a new resistance to entering a place without first collecting his thoughts, assuring himself that he won't lose anything on the way through.

Baby comes in with his arms in the confident posture he maintains even when it seems he has lost himself for a moment. He's wearing a camo-print bomber jacket, puffy around his frame, which in late years has shrunk down around the bone.

I hold out the briefcase to him.

"Anything?" he says.

"Ancestry," I said. "Again."

He nods, doesn't take the case from me. As expected, or I would have had to hide the DNA results. This has become my project. Most of Baby's life has become my project. When he started to go I felt most surprised by the lack of indignance when receiving help. He accepted immediately, handed himself over to me. Whereas before he kept some distance, locked things away. Without the boundary of his privacy, I am forced to accept his passage from life into end-of-life. Otherwise, with some kicking and screaming on his way out, I might insist that the spirit lives separate from the body.

Throughout childhood and into his early teens Baby had a recurring dream about waking up in the morning and opening his dresser drawers to find his biological parents chopped up in pieces and packed into the drawers in place of his clothes. Then this dream was replaced by one featuring his adoptive mother sitting in the antique blue-velvet

upholstered chair in the corner of his bedroom, which usually was a resting place for clean unfolded laundry. Then
the dream became one about the adoptive mother getting
up from the chair, wearing articles of his clothing, presumably articles that were in waking life left on the chair
awaiting folding and putting away, and she would walk
toward the bed and then continue walking and move right
through the bed and right through Baby too.

"Mail?" says Baby. He stands still in the centre of the
room in a way that I realize is only ever done by visitors.
At home we tend to stick to the edges.

"From the ancestry site," I say, show him the briefcase.

This time Baby holds out his hand. He puts the briefcase
on the table in the living room. I'll have to wait until he
sleeps to go in and open the letters. The problem with this
here-then-gone business is, sure, sometimes I could open a
letter right in front of him, read the contents aloud, and it
would be as though I weren't there. Other times, he watches
my every move, would request that I read it all aloud to him.

When I first moved in I had a dream that I'd gone into
the kitchen to get a glass of water and Baby's adoptive
mother was sat at the breakfast table reading one of Baby's
books—I couldn't tell which one but I just knew it was
his. I didn't get back to sleep that night, told Baby in frantic winding details. He doesn't remember his own dreams,
even when prompted. In this way perhaps he's been freed
from them. The blue-velvet upholstered chair, now in the
living room downstairs, remains empty. Neither of us ever
sits in it.

5

WE'VE GONE TO THE pier for the fish-and-chip stand. Baby fell asleep in front of the TV earlier, didn't talk much on the drive over. In my bag, two cans of cider, and a club soda to have in between. I have to decide if I'm going to tell Baby about how I've pitched the memoir, if I have the nerve. How I have to finish it quickly, and will need him to gather more notes. I'm wearing something of Pauline's, a navy twill trench coat belted at the waist. We are alone at the pier save for the man dunking battered fish in a fryer, though there are a number of parked cars whose drivers must have walked off along the main street. Should one of them return, my posture would change. For now I feel we are alone. This is the only way I am able to see what's around me. When I am watched, it is as if I see myself from the outside. My own line of vision blurs.

Two docks jut out into the bay. Seagulls pick at little things, ruffle gently in the wind. One huddles under a bench nearby, tightened into a feathered fist. My boots make a sound that I associate with my mother, clacking against the concrete parking lot. I feel self-conscious, search for somebody we might be disturbing. When I approach the food stand I walk on my toes, keeping my heels from hitting the ground. Baby goes and sits on the bench and disturbs a bird, which bobs toward the docks.

He's written some of his poems here, a couple of them prize winners. His most recent collection, *Better, More Often*, though nearly five years old now, he wrote by the water. This was near the end of his consistent lucidity. The title, retroactively, ironic.

I bring two pink bundles of food to the bench, hand him one.

Baby's face is empty. He's staring out at the water, nodding gently. He's writing, I can tell.

"Haircut Behind a Magnolia Tree," he says.

"Just now?" I say.

"Just now."

"How does it go?"

"Ah." He thinks. "There are houses along the water."

"Mm."

"Opposite the footpath. I am looking into back windows." A crease between his brows. "Thieving images from the evening."

He is displeased. "No." He shakes his head. Continues, "I see through French doors, though obscured."

"A haircut, behind a magnolia tree," I say.

"Yes." He smiles, amused. "No good."

The water is black; it'll rain later. I'll go for a drive alone once it starts to come down, pretend I'm nowhere. When

I'm away from the house I imagine things sit still. The oven clock, the sun in its position in the sky, the way long fingers of light creep under the kitchen island. In childhood I felt a constant pull toward home, as if the longer I stayed out, the more things would become rearranged, wither and die, no longer belong to me. Intentionally I left my bed unmade, put small tokens of my having been there on windowsills, under my pillows. In this way I could track the static sameness of my bedroom. I would return with a great longing for the way things were before I left. Whereas before I've often had a fear of returning to difference, now it's the pallid lull that sickens me. Pauline was the opposite. She went out and stayed out, returned home in the small hours of the morning. She had a coolness about time that I envied. She squeezed every drop out of an evening.

Baby told me a story about Mark Richman once. He hired a moving company to pack, move, and unpack his belongings all while he was at work at the agency. He ate a bowl of cereal at his old house, left the unwashed bowl on the counter, went to work, and came home to his new house, fully unpacked, and ate dinner at the same table, in a different kitchen. Returning home felt this way to me. A mood broke as soon as I left a room. This has been the great comfort of Baby's house. Moving in I felt a sense of finality. As if I would never move out. As if Baby losing things only cements them in time. Plus his world becomes increasingly smaller than mine. So, inside the house we are safe. It's only outside, especially when I drive into Toronto, that I feel on edge.

But I am only pretending, in the house. The danger comes from inside of Baby. If only it were a beast clawing at the windows, there might be something I could do.

The afternoon is coloured by my needing to work. I haven't yet today. In fact I haven't written nearly as much as I'd have liked, especially considering my meeting with Mark Richman.

I eat and drink quickly, have to sit awhile before I feel able to drive again. Baby hasn't touched his food. I fold the paper back into a little package around the battered fish, place it between us on the bench. The cider has warmed my skin, relaxed me into the idea that I might not get to writing today.

"Say it again," he says.

"You say it with me," I say. "Haircut Behind a Magnolia Tree."

"Haircut Behind a Magnolia Tree," he says, in a voice he uses when he addresses an audience. He holds his head up, looking out at the water as if it is full of eyes.

When I say "Thieving the images," I feel a sickness in my body. I am reminded of how I could see from my child-hood bedroom down the hall to the place where Baby's and Pauline's doors faced each other. The way the moonlight would illuminate the end of the hallway meant that I could see from the darkness of my bedroom and not be seen in return, should somebody look. I'd liked it this way because I feared the dark, and used the window at the end of the hallway as a nightlight. If I were to awake suddenly from a dream, sometimes I would see Baby in the doorway of Pauline's room, standing still and facing away from me.

I imagined that he was watching over her like an angel. He used to promise me, "If I die, I will be visible to you," and I imagined he'd said the same to Pauline. I asked her once a few years ago about the way that he would watch over her in her sleep, and she became angry with me, refused to talk.

"Thieving images from the evening," I say.

"I see through the doorway," he says. Hadn't it been "through French doors"? Was he now recalling the same image as I was?

"A haircut, behind a magnolia tree."

"An old woman made anew," he finishes.

"Is that the last line?"

"Could be," he says. "It's no good."

HOME. BABY IS SET up at the kitchen island with a book. The cover page is folded back so I can't see what it is. He's gotten himself a glass of iced tea, a small bowl of potato chips. I've been hoping to read to him some of what I've written in his memoir, but I've been waiting for a more lucid moment. I have maybe half of what needs to be there in the two or three introductory chapters. Almost up to when my parents met, and some flash-forward to my teen years. Some of it from my own memory. Stories of his and stories of mine.

I busy myself so I can't find the time to worry about what I'll do with myself this evening. The television is on, a Wall Street drama with the volume so low it may even be off. With the mouths moving it's possible I'm imagining the sound of the voices. Plus, Baby is reading aloud. I know the one: *House Call*. Published in 2004 by one of the big publishers before it merged with another. My mother, years ago, told me never to read it. She wouldn't say why, or maybe he told me something about how it was early work published later. That I'd be disappointed by it. Of course I read the book, immediately.

The plot detailed a female doctor whose husband revolted her. Who fed herself trial drugs in an attempt to do a number of things: to numb herself, to put herself to sleep, to cause herself relentless sexual excitement. In the final scene—I'm forgetting exactly—the husband enters her anally, she has taken an oral muscle relaxant, there is at-length description of her excreting as he removes himself from her, re-enters. I'd put the book back where I'd found it on the shelf. At dinner I ate silently, shaking. Something about the air in the room convinced me I'd been caught. That somehow by reading the book I'd taken responsibility for its perversion.

Later that year when I found myself in the shower easing my pointer finger into my anus I recalled this passage, having previously forgotten, and felt as though it had left a mark on me. I considered it unrelated that on that same evening I took a pair of stork scissors from my mother's vanity and sliced a small curved line around the contour of my developing breast.

I soon confessed to my father what I'd been doing, once or twice a month, in my parents' bedroom when they were downstairs or out of the house. Well, I told him half of the story. What I did preceding the punishment I kept to myself. Plus the pleasure cheapened the pain. I expected him to offer some sort of apology, recognize this behaviour as being his own fault, at least partially. He told me that in the nineteenth century stork scissors were used by midwives to sever the umbilical cord. There is still a pair of them in the kitchen drawer in his house. We use them to cut small loose threads from our clothes, to open delicate mail. I've been unable to deduce if he has any recollection of the significance of this pair of scissors, to me. To *us,* I used to think, though what the book had done to me, I now realize, would never be known to him.

My phone rings. It is Mark Richman:

"Three interviews!" he exclaims. "Big ones. He can talk about the new work."

"Oh," I say, and turn away from Baby. Trying to think of who I will say I am talking to, if he asks, I lose the thread of Mark's words.

". . . and New York," he is saying.

"Great," I say. "Fantastic."

I miss something else he says, about the Arthurs, about optics. Nobody wants anything to go into the book. Everyone wants to intervene before anything gets written in. Sure, it is Baby they don't trust, but I'm still the author. I still can't help but get my back up.

Various potential solutions race through my mind, fall apart when I consider them too closely. I turn back and look at Baby and, unrelated to all of his lies, I feel a feeling of sadness.

When we hang up, I make a note to myself on the back of a used Post-it and put it in my pocket. It says, *Figure it out.*

Baby is reciting an unidentifiable passage of his book in which the facade of a butcher shop is described at length. Two men meet after many years estranged, reconnect in the night. I am in a state of disbelief. Surely he will not continue on with the rest of this book. What I fear more than revisiting that late scene is having him recite the book in its entirety and the scene not being there. And so the perversion truly belonging to me, having come from inside. The punishment being made obsolete. And now, though certainly faint. I am marked by it.

Baby reads, "I had the cleaver in my hand, and I worried about what it would do."

I make an aggressive move for the kettle. Startle him. The thought of Pauline and her cupping her hands around her mug of tea gives me a chill. I do not want to bring her into the kitchen with us. I pull at the sleeves of my sweater. Each moment in this house I betray my mother and sister.

When I look at Baby in one way he is pathetic; in another way he is like a dedicated young quarterback. He practises and practises. One day he will have absorbed himself back into his body. He will be dense, muscular, produce another great work.

NOW, THE LETTERS. Making a show of tidying up, I move the briefcase from where Baby left it in the living room to his office. While I'm in there I loudly return his desk chair to where it sits tucked under his desk, open the curtains, and then with a quicker pace I unzip a small portion of the briefcase, reach in, and retrieve the letters, slipping them into the waist of my tights. I feel like a small child, and perhaps it is only memory that causes me to act with such care. It may even be that I am hoping he is aware enough that I should keep things from him. Otherwise, well.

Somebody calls from the university. The coordinator of the creative writing department, Terry, a smallish man in his early forties, newer to the department than most and with a considerable amount of patience for it. He says little, waits for me to fill in the space. He's called to tell me the hiring manager wants to offer me my position back, to tell me that the department misses me. I hadn't considered the department. Well, when I have it's been to worry I was a fool to them. I knew it was common knowledge that I'd been hired through my father's influence. Not only the name, not only the legacy, but there are annual donations of five digits. And so when I left, also for my father, it must have appeared I didn't have much agency at all.

The coordinator has a warble in his voice that makes him seem honest; he cannot manipulate himself.

"How about everything else," he asks, about how it's going.

"We manage," I say. "And you?"

"Yes, yes. We're managing. So, Hillary, do not hesitate to get in touch with us. You know, about the job. Your job. Or anything else. It's my job to answer the phone when it rings, you know."

When we hang up something feels unsaid. There is an impossibility between us. He belongs to my father. He told me when I started at the university how he had wanted to work with Baby, how it had been a letdown for him that

Baby retired before the coordinator position opened up. As some news or other hit headlines—allegations from past students, a young local writer who claims she had a two-week affair with Baby leading up to her eighteenth birthday—the department quieted about Baby, took his face off the front page of the English department website. This happened early in my time at the university, within the first six months, and when I arrived the morning after the first news broke there was a feeling of stillness in the faculty lounge. My co-workers stopped asking me how he was, stopped giving me documents to pass on to him and instead faxed them coldly without a message.

The coordinator, I noticed back then, still kept a heavily marked-up copy of one of Baby's poetry collections in his desk drawer. *Balm for Bite*, a small-press chapbook from before Baby became a bestseller. Because Mark Richman only represented Baby's fiction, he continued to publish his poetry independently for a few years, believing this tied him in some way to the Arthurs. Then Mark advised that he stop that, too, saying it was bad for sales, or bad for something.

"Terry checked in," I said, passing Baby on my way upstairs. Then, even farther from him I called, "He's doing well," disappeared into my office.

The cheques I will deposit for Baby. The letters from the DNA site and the ancestry company, should they contain anything important, I will have to spend some time before making a show of reopening them in front of Baby, and make sure he's all there. It's just I'm losing patience for telling him twice.

The DNA site has sent a letter outlining possible health risks based on Baby's genetic predispositions. It seems a joke that Alzheimer's is first on the list—he probably doesn't even remember consenting to receive the results. The word seems more striking than any other on the page, seems almost to be the first I've seen of it printed out like that. In every other instance it's been a doctor saying "memory loss," conversation surrounding the fine line between age-related change and cause for concern. Baby has been missing the appointments recently, not because he forgets, though he does, but because he refuses. Sometimes when this happens I just let him be. He seems to believe things only get worse when they are described aloud. Otherwise symptoms simmer in the background. Each day is a new cocktail of experiences, rather than a point on a graph. I must admit I've begun to subscribe to his way of thinking. The way writing the memoir makes me both tingle with excitement and feel sick to my stomach, it's as though the stories weren't true when they happened, only are now that they're being written down. In this way I almost can feel it, how it will feel when it happens to me. I shouldn't be so sure, but it is genetic.

On the next page, notification of family matches: a niece and a second cousin. There is no further information, but because both women have selected "open" profiles, there are site-provided email addresses at which they can be contacted. Surely a niece means she knows something about Baby's mother. It would be her grandmother, after all. Would have been, that is. And the cousin might know something as well. I am to email, I am not sure what to say, or how to say it. And if they want to meet Baby? A story might come out. A person finds they are genetically close to a household literary name, they arrange to meet, he is vacant, too far gone to possibly be producing work, but what's this, a new work next spring? Is it worth the risk? I send brief and friendly emails to each of the connections. I will tell him about this later. Sometime, when the time is right. I feel I am meddling and regret reaching out already. However, the two of them would have been notified of a match just the same.

6

I SEARCH FOR SOMETHING to do. There is a box of things from Pauline's apartment that belong to her ex-boyfriend. So, I am out again. Racing the evening to get to Toronto before pitch black. It starts to come so early in November. The stereo is broken; there's a jam that Baby never got to fixing, and because it predated my use of the car there's a certain permanence that I feel about it. I feel impatient with the radio. The control provided by the music streaming platforms has spoiled me. Something on CBC about a childhood in suburban Ontario. A radio documentary by a Canadian novelist about her experiences with abuse in the church. Her parents forcing her to stand naked before some religious official (she can't remember who) to do something (she can't remember what) in the realm of inspecting or possibly cleaning or even for no reason at all. The novelist speaks in the flat self-aware tone of someone practised in the art of the unaffected recital of personal statement. There is a piano track playing beneath her voice, and I hear that first, then recall certain phrases she has spoken only in memory. My brain takes them in despite my focus being elsewhere. This disturbs me, that I am powerless to language. I cannot hear words and not understand them. I cannot look at a page and not see what it has to say. The piano is light, trilly, like the pianist's right hand is on the keys and their left hand is doing something else. What else? A man's hand, I imagine. I change the station, arrive at static, and stay there. I am nearly in Toronto.

DANIEL MEETS ME OUTSIDE. He hesitates for a moment, as if he might hug me, but his arms remain stiff at his sides. He looks old to me, not like an older sister's boyfriend but like an old man. Perhaps he has always looked this way, but before, I considered us all to be so far from death. Middle age was something that only came once a person was ready for it, once it made sense, I thought. Death was something I would wake up one day and prepare for. My own, others', that is. Am I old, too? Does old mean having lived for a long time, or does it simply mean near one's end?

Daniel lives on the main floor of a triplex in the west end, with a new girlfriend. Her name is Virginie, and she hovers while we bring the box in. Daniel slices through the tape with his house key. Virginie is smoking a cigarette in the living room and I can tell from the white of the walls and the smell of the apartment that it is not a habit. An act of defiance, maybe. Her hair is tossed over to one side in a wild sort of Parisian bob. Or, I'm projecting because of her name and her accent. On somebody less debonaire the hair might look like it has just come out of bed.

I do not want to see Daniel open the box. My body reacts as if I am seeing gore when he pulls out the contents one by one, places them on the coffee table. They are his own things, but to Virginie, they are Pauline's. I know this.

Daniel is happy like a child. "My records," he says. "Ah, the coffee grinder, ah, my books," etc. I feel that this moment belongs to us, that Virginie is being a pest. She smokes her cigarette down to the filter and lights another one, refuses to sit. I am Pauline to her, too, I bet. Everything in the room that is not her own has Pauline all over it. Daniel is immersed in Pauline. I cannot blame him; everyone was. My father called her "My beautiful Pauline," raked his fingers through her long hair. He spoke to her in a way he spoke to nobody else, not even my mother. But my mother was a close second. With me he has always been matter-of-fact. I grew to appeal to him through hard work.

There is a hint of a smell in the room—I might be imagining it—coming from the contents of the box. It makes me nauseous, and I am confronted with the closeness of everything. It was not much over a year ago that I smelled that scent on Pauline's clothes, her arms around me, bringing me into her apartment, pouring cheap white wine into dollar store glasses, ordering foil plates of fried rice and General Tao chicken, eating on the floor in pairs of her girlish-patterned pyjama pants.

"Shall we have a drink?" Daniel has retrieved a bottle of scotch from the box, some expensive-looking brand I don't recognize.

Virginie pleads with me with a glance. It is on me to put a stop to this, to get my shoes on and go. "I'm driving," I offer. "Probably shouldn't."

Satisfied, Virginie looks away, smokes.

"Just one," said Daniel. "Can't hurt! To Pauline."

Oh, how tone-deaf. In a way I feel responsible for how he is in relation to Pauline. After all, I've brought her into their home. I try to communicate back to Virginie with a look that I tried my best. I am warming up to her. Reluctantly she goes to a cabinet in the next room, retrieves three glasses and brings them in on top of a big hardcover book, like a serving tray.

"Are you still over on the Danforth?" Daniel pours two generous fingers into a glass and passes it to me.

"No, not anymore."

He gives one to Virginie, then pours one for himself. His has been filled the highest.

"I'm taking care of my dad," I say, since no one has followed up.

Daniel takes a big drink, gives me a look. "I figure he can afford professional care." He seems to be more taken by the alcohol than us, and I realize he must have been drinking in preparation for my visit. "No?"

"Babe," says Virginie. The pet name seems awkward in her mouth, like she has committed to losing him for the evening. Like Pauline is in the room with us.

"He could," I say.

We finish our drinks mostly in silence. I worry Daniel might pour another round, though the alcohol has given me a certain freedom. Now I could muster a no, to be sure.

Anyway Virginie has started on dinner, which I take as my cue to leave. There is a smell of frying garlic from the kitchen, the crash of wine meeting a hot pan.

Daniel walks me to the door and his eyes are shiny. "You ever need anything . . . " He nods at me. "Okay?"

"Okay," I say.

———

IT WAS DANIEL WHO found her. In bed with her night-dress on and her mouth a thin pale line. For hours he'd thought she was sleeping, and he'd watched an episode of *The Wire* on her laptop in the living room before heading to bed. Her mouth was closed, he said. Everyone's mouth is always open when they're dead on TV. He insisted that she must have been alive when he got there, that he watched television in the next room while the time he had to save her ran out. He found vomit in the bed and a note on the desk, which ended:

"It's nothing personal,

I love you,

Pauline."

Yes, she'd known the roommate would be out. Yes, she'd known Daniel would enter using the spare key she'd given him and arrive late after his shift at the restaurant. Still, he could not accept that he was the subject to whom the letter was addressed. She would've specified, he told me.

When I think of the scene I can't help but imagine that Pauline is lying there, amused. That the click of the door was heard by her, that she felt the apartment shake when the stiff front door slammed behind him, that she lay so still trying not to be seen, barely breathing, waiting for a perfect moment to spring up and shout "Surprise!" like in games we played in childhood. She never could keep a straight face; the idea of her being anybody but herself was laughable. But Daniel left the restaurant that night and drove to the apartment, entered alone, and was alone the whole night, until authorities arrived and took the body away, and then he was alone again.

—

I TAKE A WALK the long way around the block, holding my car keys inside of my pocket. In a way, I don't want to go home, or, I don't want the wait that comes with the drive. I need a comfort more immediate than the trip back. I wonder briefly if I want sex, since my situation at home prevents it. It would seem an intrusion on my body. I haven't, not since before Pauline. Perhaps never again.

My last love, James, was a fighter; he took steroids and had these horrible outbursts. With him, I melted into a routine. He would be angry, absent; I would take the streetcar to the mall and wander past shops, buy nothing. I just needed to be far from him, to pretend I was somebody else, with a different life. When we talked I felt always like we were on the phone. Like he couldn't see my expression or pick up on the nuance of what I was saying. I spoke a little louder and clearer to him, and even then sometimes he wouldn't understand. But things continued forward; I liked having someone. I liked the way his hands were so big, they made everything in the apartment look like it belonged to a doll. What I'm trying to say is I don't have the same desire to do it again, or to let it be done to me. And for it to be better this time, I just don't have the energy.

I drive across the city, happen to pass the pharmacy where I was yesterday, without having meant to come this way. I imagine looking in and seeing myself, the other me looking out from inside. What would I think of her? What would she think of me?

On a side street at the end of the block I find a parking space, get out and pass the pharmacy again, this time on foot. I make quick eye contact with my reflection in the dark window, keep going. A few doors down is a bar.

Now that I have had the scotch I have a taste for it. I don't know much about it, about the different kinds, but I decide to have something expensive, to continue drinking to Pauline.

There are couples at two-seaters, some single clientele along the bar, mostly men in middle age. From a young brunette in pink velvet I order a pint and a glass of whiskey. She is straight-toothed, put together, and vacant in a way that seems fearless. Seated below her I feel ancient, and ugly. My wiry hair wound around itself and clipped, with raggedy pieces around my temples, the slow collapse of my cheeks beginning at the end of my twenties. I am so used to being near Baby I forget I too am aging.

At twenty-one I worked in a trendy bar on Queen West, bussing tables. I was a timid server, didn't have it in me. When men got angry, I hid from them, tried to give their tables away to the girls working front of house. One time a writer was in town touring a new novel, and I invited Baby to bring him in. They sat at the bar, their backs to me for most of the night. I felt I had to be performatively good at my job, and I moved with an urgency from table to table. Of course, I knocked a pint into a woman's lap. Her husband jumped out of his seat, stood over me with a finger in my face. Then he fell away, as if I'd used all of my power to wish him into thin air. There stood my father, having knocked him in the side of the head with his fist. Like two school boys, Baby and the touring writer scrambled out of the bar, grabbing at each other, one shoving the other out the door. "I didn't get a good look at them," I told my boss.

No time at all passes and then I am drunk, sitting so comfortably in my seat, feeling so grateful to have worn such shoes, such clothing, so as to exude sexiness. My heels are hooked over the bar along the bottom of my chair, my legs gaping open, and I am at the bar now, the server is placing another whiskey on a wrinkled cardboard coaster. I reach for it, realize it belongs to someone beside me, and withdraw my hand. Between my legs are another set of legs, a man sitting so close, laughing at what I'm saying, all of the ridiculous things I am saying. There is something powerful, masculine about how my legs are around his, his knees together, his bare naked knees underneath his well-made pinstriped slacks.

"What are you drinking," he asks me, and I tell him I don't know, that I asked for something expensive. Oh, I've revealed myself to be stupid, and now he feels he has me. There is power in his having me, too. I give myself to him. "I asked her what is the most expensive one," I say and I laugh, close to him, and I feel self-conscious that I've breathed right on his face, but I reassure myself it just smells like whiskey. Everything is whiskey. The blur of the pot lights all watery in the dimness of the bar, the hum on the inside of my head, the warmth under my skin. He orders me another expensive whiskey and tells me what it is. He knows everything.

"You are a genius," I say, and I mean to mock him, but he is excited by this.

"You are an idiot," he says, as if he intends to fuck me this way. He intends to fuck me how a genius fucks an idiot.

He is so close to me that I smell him, and he smells like something, I can almost put a word to it, and he is licking at my mouth, and he reaches for me, under my clothes, where I fear he will find I am dry. I imagine he is Daniel, excuse myself, and exit the bar before I realize he was simply nobody.

HAVING BEEN OUT AT an unusual hour makes the night palatable to me, lightens the strip of downtown that normally gives me anxiety—how it crawls with men looking for something they're not supposed to have—and makes me feel that I am among the people on the street, and not against them like I sometimes assume. Normally I hold myself with a certain fear. Some old habit left over from being criticized by my mother in childhood. Or something. I try not to play such a victim. Besides, my mother never

takes responsibility for anything intangible. So without
the admission what good is the accusation.

I decide to lean into the night, let it have me. Climbing
into my car is like an embrace, and I am cradled in the
driver's seat by the grey leather, the world through my
windshield swaying.

I am surprised at my driving, how smooth it is, how
in control I am. My head swims but my body works as
normal. The city streams by through my windows, black,
sparkly yellow, and white, a repetitive hiss with each passing car, coming in through my open window. The air is
frigid but it keeps my attention on the road.

Then, as if a punchline, I turn off of the highway and
a shriek comes in through the window and fills the car.
I've crashed, I think to myself, feeling the sway in my seat
and wondering if it's the alcohol or if the vehicle is careen-
ing across the road. I open my door, vomit onto the road
below. Surely I've just grazed the guardrail, but the car is
banged up in this ugly way. It has a dent and these scratches
all around it where the paint has worn off. I have a pain in
my neck from the snap of the car stopping, but when I try
to recall the moment itself, it is gone. I exist in the blur of
the aftermath, the moment itself a fiction I try and fail to
recreate for myself, try to embellish with less responsibility.
As far as I can see there is no one else on the road, so I take
a big breath of outside air and get back into the car. How
stupid. How very, very stupid.

Home is a far enough drive away that I worry I will
make another stupid error if I go. Closer is Catherine's, so
I drive slowly and pull into the end of her driveway. When

I pull up she is out on the porch. It must be quite a bit past midnight now. She is like a permanent structure or lawn ornament. So rarely do I drive past and not see her there with a drink and a book, wrapped in wool with the ember of a cigarette like an eye in the dark. We are tunnelling deeper into the darkness of winter; I imagine I will find her there in the new year with piles of snow on her head and in her lap.

Catherine sits on the porch and watches the light change and the sporadic small-town back road traffic, and doesn't wither or shake the way I do when I am out for too long and my blood sugar drops. In observation, others don't seem to have the nagging physical needs that I do, but of course that cannot be true. Though time and time again I see others ignore the pull of their bodies' whims. I see girls waiting for the Orillia night-shuttle bus in groups, shrieking, their clothing effortlessly draped, worried about things like not having enough to do before morning, misplacing a belonging. Of course, I project. These same girls crawl in daylight into the pharmacy, grey dust of makeup under their eyes, some things they're able to take a pill for, others they're not. I am nobody to look at them in any which way. My body curls inward, cramps, pinches my vision into a narrow tunnel. It doesn't adapt, and it needs comfort, routine. It needs to be home.

Catherine stands up in the beams of my headlights, seems startled then recognizes the Jeep and jumps like a young girl, waving her arm over her head. "Hillary!" she yells. Her long hair is in a braid, which sways with her movement.

I turn off the car before she gets close enough to see the damage. I don't know what she'll do if she smells the alcohol on me, so I light up one of Baby's cigarettes from the glove compartment, take a long drag as I approach her.

"I'm sorry to just show up," I say. She throws herself around me, rocks our bodies side to side. She is drunk, too.

"I'm always up," she says. "I don't sleep. I'm happy to have company."

She's got the dogs, I can tell, because there's a sock monkey at her feet in the snow. I am put on edge by the sign of a dog—she walks and boards professionally, sometimes has multiple, sometimes none, but most often she boards one full-time, whose owners seem always to be somewhere distant and glamorous (Paris, London, Milan) and whose temperament is one of chaos. A violent mouth in the house.

My posture is stiff. My knowledge of the animal hardens me.

Through the week she boards a pack of them, walks them all the way into town each morning and evening with their leashes looped onto a belt around her waist. When they get excited she is like a carousel; they run after one another around her, and she spins to keep their leashes from tangling.

"I kissed someone," I say, and I feel giddy letting it spill out of me, but I see that Catherine looks severe. I continue, quieter, "I let a man kiss me. I didn't even know him."

"Men will do anything if you let them," she says.

I nod. Lesson learned.

A bark like a cough from inside.

The dogs present a challenge in their animacy and unwillingness to conform with the things people think are naturally best. Perhaps a challenge to beliefs more than standards. Though out loud I am easier on them than I feel inside. Should I speak negatively about them, I would alienate myself from Catherine. She is closer to the dogs than to any human. She sees them as perfect in their honesty, their inability to manipulate. I might too, if I didn't always have such a feeling that they are on to me.

"Can I stay with you?" I say, and surprise myself with the bluntness of my question.

She brings me in without a word. She has a pitcher of something alcoholic on the kitchen table, hands me a juice glass and fills it in my hand. I am embarrassed about having dressed up. I see Catherine's comfort, her cotton pants and grey wool sweater, and it seems obvious. What kind of woman am I trying to be?

I am thinking about my mother. How she will see the damage to the vehicle, accuse me of being out of control, of being on a path to destruction. She will ask if I was drinking, compare me to Baby. I will ruin her holidays with evidence of my recklessness. And her husband, how he will wear a look of quiet sadness on his face. This is the only way I have seen him, since Pauline. He so solemnly arrived at the funeral, said nothing, left early and came back later to pick up my shaking mother.

Catherine and I sit cross-legged on her living room rug with our backs against the sofa. She is reading an article from a lifestyle magazine detailing a woman's experience developing an empowered sense of sexuality after being abused in childhood by her father. She reads flatly—she is just reading. No matter the words, she is at home, drinking warm whiskey and lemon, whereas I have begun to lift off somewhere.

During a paragraph in which the woman explains how her father worked in manual labour, would arrive home from work—this is years after the abuse tapered off—and request that she massage him, or bandage some injury or other, and she would feel needed, flattered, something in the realm of relief, I begin to hyperventilate.

I have to wonder if she's chosen the passage on purpose. Does she think I am here because of Baby? Surely not. She looks up to him like he is some sort of hero. But why, then?

I cannot shake a series of images from my mind: Pauline returning home from her first semester of university, Baby drinking too quickly at dinner, an excited energy in the room, but when he stood to get another drink he tripped over his own feet, injured something, maybe his knee? And Pauline insisted on fixing him up. He'd not been pay-ing much attention to her prior, but submitted when she approached with a small medical kit from the bathroom. "Just let me," she'd whispered harshly, when he withdrew his leg at the sting. Slowly they eased back into their old rapport. He touched her hair in that way; she'd grown it out again, long and straight down her back. His hand down from the crown of her head to where her back curved in above her waist.

When these things happened, whatever these things were, I would slink into my mother's office. You see, each of my parents had one, one on the main floor (where

Baby's current office is) and one upstairs (where mine is now). My father's, being on the main floor, was sometimes used as a social area when entertaining guests, but mostly he did his writing in there, hung his awards on the walls, photographs of himself and other notable figures, and the like. He had a bookshelf full of just his own books, copies and copies of them. And my mother's office, well, it was used for other things. Sometimes she slept in there, or I did. Sometimes I hid in there when I was mad, closed the door and lay on the floor, sometimes I even, I think, I may have gone in there and played imaginary games of kissing, touching, may have brought myself to orgasm. But mostly I sat with my back against the door, arms around my knees, and listened to the sounds of the house in complete darkness, the world moving and moving around me. Each memory of Pauline concludes in that room, alone, drowning out the sounds of the house by will, sinking into the darkness, freezing time, and then I cannot remember another thing.

I feel now as if the alcohol has left my system altogether, in a way abandoned me.

There is an audible sound when I try to catch my breath. Catherine reaches for my hand and with my other I knock over my drink. Some pours out before she grabs it, turns the glass back upright.

"No mind," she says, rubbing her hand over my back. I barely feel it through the thick fabric of my sweater. For a moment I wish she would touch me, skin to skin, and I feel disturbed. She squeezes her arms around me and waits until my breathing slows again. I feel like I am faking it.

The dog comes up from the basement, presumably having been awoken by the racket up in the living room. It presses its muzzle all rubbery against the coffee table, locates me, and sniffs at my legs.

I make an effort not to look; he'll know. An old yellow dog used to come to the back door of the house when I was a child and Baby taught me that baring one's teeth at a dog will cause it to feel threatened and so with the protection of the glass between us I would growl at the thing, sometimes just stand still and grin, and it would snarl and gnash its teeth in the air. I worried one day it would catch me outside, remember me.

Catherine pats the dog's back with a heavy hand. "Hello, old paint," she says.

I offer a hand to the dog. He sniffs timidly, seems to accept me, and curls between us. The warmth of him pressed against my hip softens me.

Catherine turns the magazine upside down to conceal the article she'd been reading. A gesture of apology? Perhaps she'd been trying to push me in one direction or another into some sort of great confession. And perhaps she has changed her mind about it being her place. I feel consumed by her touch, and I want to do the routine again: to have her push me and then bring me back, better than before.

We finish our drinks in silence, which feels like an offering to the dog. If he can't speak, then we won't either. My eyes are heavy. I try to count how many hours I've been drinking and I keep getting stuck at the bar, unable to remember when I got there or how many drinks I ordered,

who the man was who sat down beside me and ordered
something bitter for both of us.

We sleep upstairs huddled together under an orange and
brown quilt, with a space heater in the doorway. The smell
of Catherine's skin, like baby powder and linen and something, oh, hormonal, is everywhere in the bed, and stronger
in the crook of her neck where I find myself in a half-asleep
haze. By morning we are apart again, bodies on either side
of the bed, facing away.

UNTITLED MEMOIR
By Baby Davidson

Chapter I

New York!

The city roared with life. And what a city! What is there to
say about the place that hasn't been said before, by generations
of greats before me? I shuffled from one side of the back seat
to the other and back again, drinking in the panorama that
rolled all around the windows of the taxicab. The streets were
aglow with yellow, red, neon rainbows of light. People sat dining in restaurant windows, nervous women in low-cut dresses
and hopeful men fumbling with their wallets. Young gradu-
ates over-pouring glasses of wine in dives, playing a new and
ill-fitting maturity. Jewellery in glass displays, sequins on young
dresses, expensive watches on expensive men, all shimmering
with the thrill of spring.

New York City!

Sure, I'd been, but not like this.

I was launching the first big one. A campus novel, *V
Formation*. It had always before been a small affair, a few bookstores around Toronto, maybe Montreal if there was some
extra budget. Small teams of editors held everything together in
panicked spurts of late-night work, surviving on grant money
and donations. Trust funds and side gigs, some of them. The
big international conglomerate publisher—need a hint?—had
picked up my manuscript in what we in the industry call a
Significant Deal. My agent, Mark Richman, had an expensive
bottle sent with the first portion of my advance. The cheque was

more than enough for a year, and, I was told, there was more where that came from. Now that's something, no? An advance so big it had to be drawn and quartered.

I admit there had been some romance to putting my previous three-figure advances toward my bachelor-apartment rent cheques, sharing an Olde English 800 with the Arthurs hidden away in one of the graduate offices on campus. But with my recent assistant professorship the glamour of the American book tour felt an appropriate upgrade.

Speaking of the Arthurs, there had been radio silence in the grad office when I'd told them of the news. The promotion, that is. I hadn't even gotten to the book deal. For now, good riddance!

Two of my students were to meet me at the hotel bar shortly after my arrival at noon. I'd extended the offer should they wish to gain some perspective on the industry, and, admittedly, to have some company. With nothing to do and nowhere to be, we saw no reason not to get down to business: a drink.

The hotel bar was lit up with a ceiling full of hanging gold cards, reflecting the light, twinkling like stars, or like what stars must look like in heaven. Penny, on my left, was telling a story of how she had been begged to enter the MFA, how she had actually had plans to move to Chicago and study screenwriting. Frederique was on my other side.

"The program sends you to L.A. It's a guaranteed internship," she'd said. "In the *industry*."

I ordered a round of whiskeys, on the rocks, and the girls requested the addition of soda and slices of lemon. So be it. I felt charmed by their every desire. When the waiter returned, we ordered heaping platters of club sandwiches and fries, and stuffed ourselves while we read the dessert menu like it was a good book.

It wasn't until our plates were replaced by a little black leather bill holder that we were reminded of such frivolous things as time, place, and obligation.

In the cab on the way to the venue, I sat between the girls, my knees touching one of each of their knees. The clashing scents of their perfumes and lotions and the smells that naturally float around a woman had me in a daze. There I was, their professor, drawing the curtains to reveal a window into their dreams. I felt so alive I wished I could live my entire life in anticipation. I'd felt similarly each time one of my books was going to print. I almost feared seeing it, holding it in my hands. It was a feeling of dread I knew to expect even before my first book, having seen it happen to older more storied writers. But I'd always chalked it up to their being trapped in the copycat city of Toronto. I'd thought all we needed was to shrug off the flat, dry prairies, the charming nautical Atlantic provinces, like an ugly old hand-me-down coat. I felt that certainly things would be different this time around. Though, wouldn't it have been just wonderful if the cab had never arrived?

We entered the venue as a threesome, late. The host was stalling and grinned at the sight of us. Mark Richman's shoulders relaxed, and his scolding look seemed in good humour. Really, no one seemed to mind our lateness. In fact, it titillated them, I'd say. We turned heads like celebrities. I was glad the girls were seeing me in this new light, out from under the bleak shade of the institution, out of my starched business attire, no longer responsible for leading, for cultivating a fair and professional experience, for fostering young minds. Now, I sat back and allowed myself to be experienced.

The reading was all a blur. A success! But a blackout. I regained consciousness when the soles of my shoes were back on floor level with the audience. There were hands to shake, drinks to clink, women in silk and fur, dark lipstick and dark shadow on their eyes.

Everyone wanted to discuss the inspiration behind the work.

Everyone wanted to discuss my family.

I accepted drink after drink out of the hands of strangers. The room embraced me. For this one night, I was king. The novel had real weight. The Significant Deal had been announced on Publishers Marketplace, and those who knew, knew. I felt willing to trade the bulk of the rest of my life for this night. I felt able to coast for the remainder of my years on the knowledge that I'd had this night. That I'd made it. Then, later, I'd be quiet and write. There would be infinite material in the richness of that moment on that night.

My body felt light and infinite. I wanted to talk, laugh, and fuck.

Mark Richman was introducing me to some corporate higher-ups and I found I was unable to keep with them for long enough to catch the thread of the conversation. I agreed to some things that excited my agent very much. I looked around the room for my girls and saw Frederique alone by the bar, and moved to her side.

I placed my hand on her back and felt the moisture bleeding through the silk of her slip dress. If not for that I'd have assumed she was perfectly at ease. I'd been watching her move through the room with confidence, shaking some hands of her own. Every now and again I would rejoin her, whisper something close to her ear, and smell her perfume.

She had been going along with it all night until something shifted in her—perhaps one too many—and she became very messy and unbecoming. She started to go on about my having been *scheming* all semester. I hadn't even broached the subject of bedding her. Perhaps it'd been implied by the invitation to begin with—so I'd erred.

"It's like trying to hold a beach ball underwater," she'd said, lamenting the male sex drive.

I spent a moment or two debating whether to go try my luck with Penny, whose gaze was sober and fixed on me from across the room, but didn't want to risk souring my mood with another talking-to. In any case it's always better dreamed of than done.

Back in my hotel room, alone, I drifted in and out of sleep, surveying the events of my life. I remembered my parents, teaching me how to speak, to read, to write. I thought, how magnificent that it had all turned out this way. I remembered my childhood friends, my feeling of uselessness among my peers. I thought of the first time I purchased sex—oral—from a prostitute, at fifteen. I remembered how her body hadn't looked how I'd thought a body would look. It was imperfect, human, maternal, and I couldn't get hard.

Sleep wouldn't come. There was more life to live. Excitedly, with a jittery wakefulness, I hailed a cab to the airport and made my way home, wearing the scent of the best night of my life. To have slumbered, to have woken in the stark morning light through the cheap hotel curtains . . . I simply could not risk spoiling the perfection of the trip with one unremarkable moment. The sun cast a dull pink glow over the city, threatening to turn the page.

7

A REPORTER FROM A big American magazine calls requesting Baby. "He's working," I say. "This is work," she pushes back, and I do not know what to tell her. I resent Mark, who surely gave the reporter our number. The top rim of my glasses across my line of vision cuts off Baby's head so that I can only see his still, small body perched in his chair. Reminiscent of the cover of *Sword & Stone*'s "Beheading Issue." Later, I tell her, he'll be available for interview. She is impatient with me, probably assumes I am some young fling. She offers me a deal: later today, or it's off.

So, we get to work. Baby by the entrance at the phone table on the landline, and I call him from my cellphone in the kitchen. The back of him is in clear view to me. Hunched over the table, holding the phone receiver in both hands, now he looks bigger than usual, like some sort of house-trained monster.

"Hi, this is so and so from the most esteemed literary journal on the planet. Am I speaking with Baby Davidson?"

There's a pause. He turns to look at me, then turns back. He's been training for this. "Speaking," he says.

"So there have been rumours about a forthcoming release. What can you tell me about the work?"

"Well," he says. He has before him two of his books and a stapled collection of notes on pages torn from a legal pad. He puts his hand flat on one of the covers. I worry he'll fumble. And if he does when it's just him and me, then . . .

He goes on. "Not a whole lot, so and so."

I laugh, but it is staged. It's all part of the game.

"You know how this business works. If I tell you the truth it won't be true by the time it hits the stands." This is rehearsed. Originally from a phone interview with another magazine, years ago. This line was cut but the recording was given to him by an intern. Seemed against the rules somehow but it was never said that this was explicitly against company policy. So, we poach what we can from the unreleased recording. He's heard laughing at that point, pauses, goes, "Can't say a whole lot about too much. Won't be true tomorrow if I say it today."

"How has your writing process changed as you've entered this new stage of your life and career?" Blindsiding him. She will too, so I'm not just digging.

Baby rubs at one arm, pulls at the small white hairs. He looks like a boy. In photos from his childhood, there is something in his face that he looks to have grown out of in adulthood but that sometimes returns now in old age. A fear, or something else exposed and painful. Kids got thrown into the water then, he's told me, and he just drowned. He developed a habit of pulling hairs from his eyebrows, eyelashes, later into adolescence his arms so as to be less conspicuous, not to wear the habit on his face. Strangely, in late years, he has more or less stopped, unless markedly lucid. He drops the habit when he's forgetting, as if losing so much of himself that he is freed too of anxiety. A lifetime of routine panic erased from the brain, leaving the body unfamiliar and with too little to do. Although it's not as if a strength returns in its place. The frame has been exhausted.

So, he must be in there now. He uses his thumbnail against the tip of his pointer finger, grips, and pulls. When he snatches a hair, he presses it to his lips to feel it, then brushes it away somewhere. It has served its purpose as a small pinprick of sensation.

"Mr. Davidson," I say. "Dad."

"Well it's become difficult," he says to me, phone receiver placed ear and mouthpiece down on the telephone table. "What with my, ah, my difficulties, with my, ah . . ."

He's gone off script. Clearer than usual, and I almost want to end the game, get as much out of him as I can before he goes again.

What did you do to her, what did you do? I am shaken by an image of myself shrieking. I see him standing in the doorway in the night. There's a sudden heat in my body. An anticlimactic nausea. There is validity in my feeling of sickness so long as Baby is in the room with me. Then, when he forgets again, it is as if I lose the moment, too. We will be new, strange people. I take care of him on principle; he follows my lead because he doesn't have the awareness to consider doing things any other way. This dynamic mimics my childhood, with the roles reversed. I feel distracted, can't get too far into any of that. Sometimes I go so far as wondering if the forgetting is an illusion, or at least a mechanism of self-preservation. If one day he realized who and what he is and it overwhelmed him to the point of sacrificing his entire person, severing his engagement with the world. This, I've discussed briefly, unspecifically, with my mother. "Think of it as a death," she said. "That person is gone now."

"I thought we weren't going into the memory, eh Dad? Not yet at least."

"Ah, well . . ."

I go to the cupboard and get a rocks glass, inspect its bottom for dust. Pour two fingers of whiskey and the left-over third of a can of club soda Baby has in the fridge. When he hears the sound of the ice cubes clinking, he turns.

"Yes, please," he says.

He hasn't had a drink in the time I've been living here with him. Once or twice in the past few years I've seen him sip a glass of wine with dinner, if it's placed in front of him. But since the night my mother left him, he hasn't gone back to it.

The year my parents got divorced, in my early teens and Pauline's late, my mother wrote out a list of every way my father ever wronged her and read it out to the family at dinner. I strain to remember a single item on the list and can't. I remember Pauline carrying on eating while it happened, serving herself second and then third helpings of food, as if threatening my mother, *You keep going and*

I'll keep going. My father sat at one end of the table and
with each list item he began to smile and then laugh, and
by the end of the list he was howling.

I pour him one too, bring it to him.

"So, Mr. Davidson," I say, emboldened somehow by the
weight of the drink in my hand before I've even sipped it.
"How do you feel about the ethics of writing about family
in a memoir?"

Baby considers the drink in his mouth for a moment,
then swallows. "I gave myself away long ago."

"To literature?"

"To the world."

This means nothing to me. Sometimes, when I am par-
ticularly frustrated with him, my whole body seems to itch.

"Mr. Davidson," I say, "do you feel you've done damage
to others?" I am surprised, myself, at the question. I do
want him to feel the pain that waits for him in his recollection. I do. "Your daughters?"

His hands are still for a moment. Then he's arranging
objects on the telephone table, moving them to a new place
and then moving them back. Gone again.

"Charlie Rose!" he says, breaking me out of some spell.
The sounds of the room filter back into my awareness:
fridge hum, living room clock, a ringing in my ears since
childhood. My mother has it too, the tinnitus, and can't be
alone with it. When my parents were still sharing a bed my
mother would wake him up in the night, frantic, tell him it
was so loud it was physically hurting her. She'd beg him to
listen harder to the silence in the room, to tell her he could
hear it too. Sometimes make him hold his ear right up

against hers. Eventually he started to, continues to claim to this day—when aware—that he hears it, insists that somehow she gave it to him. That she suggested it so many times that he hears it louder than anything else, piercing through the air in the house and making him forget. "It's not memory loss, it's distraction," he's told me. "It's your mother." Decidedly, I think of something else. "Charlie Rose," he says. "Nineteen ninety-six. Baby Davidson on his new collection of short stories."

"Alright," I say. "Come get set up on the iPad."

THINGS EASE BACK. The cheapness of the sound through the device's speaker almost like an old radio. Heavy snow outside, stacked on the windowsills and decorating spruces in the backyard. Waffled over the backstop in the baseball field. In the distance, the bay is dark and frothing across the top of small waves. Quietly, just under the sound of Charlie and Baby in conversation, I put on *The Perry Como Christmas Album*. It's his favourite. The image of winter consumes me, puts me in a state of ease around my father again, in remembering holidays in childhood. My mother was impartial, did her part in the routines when called for. Baby pushed for keeping up with tradition. The oranges, the unwrapping first thing in the morning, cocoa and confectioner's sugar in brown instant packets. It was this time of year when Baby was content, and the contentment meant he would sit quietly in his office, just off the living room, and write letters to his friends, to other writers, and leave us alone. Oh, I shouldn't say *us*. Sure, I got knocked for screwing up—a bit of silent treatment for a bad grade, a harsh word or two if I talked back—and I had to take care of Mom when she was hurt or keep her company when Catherine or another woman was over in the house. But Pauline was the one who'd been left alone with him all those times. "Daddy time," he called it, when they would spend time together just the two of them. To make up for the fact that I'd come along and robbed Pauline of her attention. Or, well, that's what I'd figured.

Baby—the other one, in the interview—is talking about a female reader mailing him her hair. I turn up the music and Perry Como drowns him out.

Growing up I didn't have an understanding of fame. Baby got to talk about himself on TV, got stopped in bookstores sometimes and scribbled his name on the title page of his books. People never could seem to believe he would just walk around in bookstores like a regular person. It always was funny to me that somebody would be so excited to see my dad when I saw him every day, in his undershirts and old gym shorts. There were pictures in his office of him and other men my parents referred to as geniuses. So, I thought that he and Perry were one in the same. I imagined when he travelled for conferences, book tours, and the like, that he was among all other famous men—Jesus, Kafka (funny, that's who was "famous" in our house)—scale and context only partially formed for me.

Now, with some perspective, I see the smallness of the writer when left alone. And what happens when he forgets for good? The readers don't want the same repeated words. They have the books; they've fleshed them out in graduate school classrooms, endnoted his genius, accused him of misogyny ("A rite of passage for the literary man!" he told me). He sits in the kitchen and memorizes his lines, his face, his disposition. He becomes more and more just another reader of himself. He only has so many conversations left in him before the press realizes he is an actor playing his past. Before it comes out that Baby Davidson has died, and that his namesake is dying with him. His eldest ate poison, his other is useless. Can't produce a sentence worth reading.

I'll have to try harder with the memoir. Oh, to be a Davidson and have nothing to show for it.

If it is not too late already, it will be soon. I will turn things around. I will write the second half this week.

Baby says, "It's just a classic kinda book, you know. Nothing fancy." He laughs.

I do a sweep of the room. Perk up some pillows, pass the record player so I can turn up the Perry Como album. I imagine us—me and Perry—at the dark table in the *Charlie Rose* studio. *Yes, it's all true,* I tell him, *the Pauline parts.* Perry smiles the same friendly-eyed smile he's doing on the cover of the LP. It's Christmas, we're drinking hot cider out of studio-logoed mugs. Studio employees are adjusting our clothes, offering a selection of items. Snow is falling, either still or again. Snow is somehow indoors, outside of the boundaries of what is visible on-screen. Blanketing over studio equipment.

I fix myself another drink, and another for him too.

Out back, the sloping yard is soft through the static of snow, the line of vision limited to the dark green of tree

needles, the darkness of the water, the red door of the
shed. But far in this direction the bay opens out and meets
the other side where the empty rental cottages sit under
sheets of snow, teeth of ice along their troughs. Behind the
cottages, a road to town, a highway leading to the big city,
where work after work of brilliance is produced, stocked
on shelves, hung in galleries. Here, not so much goes on.
I wipe a streak through the fog on the window, bringing a
layer of darkness through. The view intensifies. My illusion of Toronto fades behind the flurry, and I am alone,
distant. Baby has stopped reciting, only listens now, and
in 1996 he and Charlie Rose clink their mugs together in
appreciation of an in-joke poking fun at The Business,
from their positions at the top.

I want to snatch the glass from his hand. But what holds
me back is the humanness of the action. I haven't touched
him with intention in any recent memory. Perhaps to steady
him while he gets up, I might offer my elbow. But to take
something away from him, to look him in the eye like I am
some evil mother, I just couldn't. I've often wondered how
I'll cope when things worsen, which they will. At present
he bathes himself, dresses himself. We sit adjacent to each
other in the kitchen, talk mostly with our backs turned,
did it that way before any of this, before I moved in.

When I was fifteen he told me, "This is the age when
girls stop hugging their fathers." He'd said it with a sadness that seemed to be asking me for something. But he
was right. I never did it again.

There may have been moments we made a joke: a
handshake upon departure, like old business partners.

Otherwise we keep a distance that causes me anxiety, by contrast, when we are forced into close quarters. When we drive, for example, I feel aware of our legs. I feel self-conscious when I have to crane my head past him to look out of the passenger window. As if he might think I am looking at him, trying to connect.

So, to act suddenly and aggressively would be twofold: the obvious, but also some sort of withdrawal from our established posturing. Reverting to a time much different from now.

In my childhood he would put on Little Richard's "Tutti Frutti" and we would dance in the living room. He'd have me up in the air in his hands in such a way so as to secure me, so that I could not fall, but could not get out willingly either. His hands under my shirt to grip my bare skin. We would turn in circles, dizzy, together, then I would kick my legs and he would let me down, laugh at how I tried to steady myself, walking drunken circles around the area rug.

I don't want to be having thoughts.

I remember this scene because it is featured in one of his short stories, "Dancing on the Head of a Pin." And because of this I don't know how to distinguish the memory from the writing. It is possible it never happened at all. Reading about this memory of his—what he takes note of, what his perspective is on me—makes me feel invaded. Moment by moment it can be assumed a person is occupied with other things. That interactions are unaffecting. To think back and remember his watchful eye plagues me.

In part I am kidding myself. I must admit I want him to have the drink. Then another, even. I consider that there might be something inside of him that will be unlocked by the alcohol. I am able to move forward with unethical tasks if only I tell myself they are for Pauline.

For Pauline, I will do whatever it takes. I will hide her small truths in his story and she will take shape among the pages, emerge like a pop-up, come face to face with the reader. Then, they will know. Then, his story will be concluded. Baby will not end with his death, but with the release of his (*his*—ha!) final work. The truest thing about him, the core of him, was what he did to her, what I know but cannot put to words. But I will. And with the unleashing of her truth, it will be understood that he died when she died. She is the only one who saw him for who he was in his entirety, the monster who lived between their bodies. I will make this clear.

8

AT NIGHT I AM unable to sleep. I am wide awake with guilt, having poured drink after drink for my father. Really it got me nowhere. I try to recall Pauline from memory. Her essence. Surely I am changing it, distorting it, in my recollection. Her emails alone were better prose than I am able to write with hours at the desk. Pauline could say anything about anything and it would be in the most simple, beautiful way. I on the other hand ramble on, choose the wrong words, and too many of them. She had such a coolness about her, even more so on the page. I am too taken by emotion to ever be a powerful writer.

I try to touch myself but there is no feeling between my legs. Ever since I lost Pauline, I think of her any time I try to go there. It's not like that; I think of her when I do anything. But she was all I knew about that sort of thing. I mimicked her to conceal my boyishness, my disconnection from my own body. I took from her just like everybody else.

"My beautiful Pauline," Baby would say. Every night he brushed her hair. It was delicate and knotted easily, and so long. He would pull the brush down nearly to her waist and she would whine. When I was young I would ask why not mine. "It's too curly," he said. "It doesn't brush."

One evening Pauline arrived at the dinner table with her hair chopped up above her shoulders. It made her look like a woman, the blunt yellow-blonde bob. She'd done it with craft scissors in her bedroom. "Cool, eh?" she laughed, shaking her hair for us.

Baby, furious, emptied his glass of wine and placed it in front of her. Retreated to his writing desk for the remainder of the evening. In the morning, he was sweeter to me. Seemed to be trying me out, but became bored. In time he forgave Pauline.

I try to ease my way into it, beginning over top of my cotton underwear.

I think about how Pauline must have been afraid of Baby. Stupidly, I did nothing. Either that or she felt shut out by how he favoured me. Favoured me by sparing me, that is. Yes she was more like him, charismatic and talented, and he doted on her. But he let me be.

I'm not afraid of Baby and never was. Perhaps it is because I live inside the world he built for me. So to be without him would be more frightening than any one thing he could do.

Sometimes I almost feel that losing Pauline was a blessing, insofar as my relationship to her. It is as if in a way she protected us. To see someone deteriorate, and I'm speaking of Baby of course, seems to me a much worse thing to witness than to lose them when they are young. The progression of my mother aging, for example, is so severe due to the distance. Each time I see her I am shocked.

My father used to say "Everyone is somebody else's asshole," and about my mother, he once said, "The asshole in our relationship was both of us." At times I've gone through the motions of imagining they had both realized earlier, parted amicably. Of course then I wouldn't be, well, anything. But for the sake of the exercise . . .

Would I have been normal otherwise? I've always assumed I'm made of flimsy and flawed things, that this is who I am and so best to take advantage of it. But to think I might have had a chance at normalcy. Had I come only from my mother. It's as if I'm experiencing anger for the first time. All those years ago a therapist said, "Doesn't that make you angry?" and I said, " . . . I don't know what you mean."

Sometimes now I sit in bed and pretend to be Pauline. Still and straight with my head on the hard pillows, two of them stacked. I pretend I am too upset to be doing anything else and I wait for someone like me to bring me my breakfast and usually at that point I fall back asleep. I could never pull off the finesse of depression. I always would creep downstairs and get up to something. Distract and lose half the day to inspiration. But just as sad as anything.

So little happens in this house, but so much has happened in the past. The walls seem to vibrate and hum with what they've seen.

9

THE APPROACH OF CHRISTMAS presents a challenge: appease my mother without leaving Baby on his own. The thing is, I regret to say, I was not expecting things to continue this way into the dead of winter. The decline of his mental functions brought about talk of professional care, or worse. His (they call themselves) support team advised I might plan to be there with him for the fall season, expect my life to be my own again thereafter. He does continue to go, but his body is healthy enough.

The reporters, the publishers, the readers, seem to be a growing swarm. Yesterday even, a neighbour cut through the yard and told me she saw an article, asked about the book. They all want something from him, and maybe I want the same thing. Answers, confessions. They want more work, they want him to keep the old work alive by producing new work. There is a pressure to always be moving.

Baby does do his own writing. It's just that if anyone were to see what he's really producing things would be even worse than if he never publishes again. I go through his files sometimes while he sleeps. It's easier for me to write at his desk, as though I'm taking some of his energy from him. But the work is frightening in its incoherence. Some of it so severely fragmented it is as though he typed randomly and without looking. Other parts begin to sound like him, how he used to sound, but break off, lose their cohesiveness. In some places there is no sense of grammar or punctuation. One page for example reads:

I am the rat held between the watchmaker's forceps.

Watch out: ! The watchmaker is in.

A, aa, aaa.

Other parts seem almost copied down from somewhere. There will be pages and pages of phrases like, *And then he put the pedal to the metal* and *Well, he said, it takes one to know one!* Occasionally I ask him how his work is going. He says, "It's going."

The more the days bleed into each other, the less that happens, the more I am beginning to feel moments from before. I am interrupted drinking my coffee by the recollection of a certain room in my Toronto apartment, from a certain angle. The way the potted palm's clawlike shadow stretched across the wall in early evening, the books stacked in jagged piles all around the armchair, the windowless bedroom with a sharp turn at its entrance, so when viewed from outside it appeared to be a door opening up to a blank wall.

I am hit by other, farther things, too. Childhood toys I shared with Pauline. The sickly smell when she did my makeup for me before we were allowed. She first did mine, then her own, and we stood in the front window in my bedroom and looked down at the road, hoping somebody might walk by and look up to see two pretty women.

These are things I may never have returned to. I must wonder how much a person forgets. See, with Baby, the forgetting takes up space. He misplaces, he is confused, he cannot answer an ordinary question. "How have you been," someone will say, and he will take on a look as if to say, "When?" But this other forgetting, in all of the secrets we keep from ourselves, happens without our knowing. A person should need an extra year for everyone in their life, just to reflect. Now all I have is time. Now it is just myself and my life. Surely I could live out the rest of my time going over and over what has already happened.

I am racing against the progression of Baby's memory loss, to finish the first draft of the memoir. You see, the audience cannot suspect that he is too far gone to have written something. I crawl through his old notebooks, files on his computer, sticky notes in haphazard piles.

In one of his old notebooks, a poem titled "Children":

I was not born
Really, I just appeared
All of a sudden, just like that
And as I came into being,
I will one day die.
So too will my name.

The poem is dated, 12 April 1983. Pauline would have been around two years of age. I should note the whole poem is struck through with a line, and a note that says, *Bad*.

So, my mother. I have not spent a Christmas without her in more than thirty years. But, see, neither had Pauline.

For me to miss this year what with Pauline and everything would cause irreparable damage, I imagine. It is true that last Christmas was the first in actuality. We let it go. It passed us by, a blur, colourful lights on all of the houses strung up, turned on, turned off, taken down.

If we wake up early, we can have Christmas at the house. Then, if I leave before noon, I will make it to my mother's in time for a late lunch, some catching up, dinner and gifts, and then home to fix things up at Baby's. Perhaps a second dinner with him, if he is lucid and insists. I never did learn how to cook, not for anything like a holiday. Everyone else just seems to know. Pauline would arrive full-bodied and red-lipped, with chunky fashionable rings on her fingers, passing out plates of something she found in the *New York Times*. Nordic-looking cookware right out of a magazine.

TODAY BABY WANTS TO go to the lot behind the church and get our Christmas tree. It'll be too heavy for us, I tell him, but he cannot be swayed. Plus he has some interview over the phone, and if he is tired he is more likely to get confused. We already missed the other one, with some other prestigious publication. I am trying to stall and wait for him to be struck by a different idea, so I can be alone. I really must get back to the memoir, and get something substantial to Mark Richman. He'll start calling soon if I don't. I've already burned through two of the seven days I gave myself to complete the draft.

Baby is dressed in an old pair of jeans that sag at the knees, with frayed string around the bottom hem, and a

thick blue-plaid coat made of wool. He is ready to go. In
addition to the compulsive nervous behaviours that Baby
engages in when he is more aware, he is also reminded of
the temptation to smoke cigarettes. And so today, quite in
his own mind, he smokes in the car with the window down
just about an inch. Cold wind whistles through the gap,
blowing most of his smoke back in toward us. I like the
smell of smoke in the winter, hate it in the heat.

In summer growing up I would move some of my things
down into the basement, sleep on the old futon by the back
brick wall. It was cooler down there and the two outlets
within reach of my bed in my upstairs bedroom didn't
work, so there was no convenient way to have a rotary fan
in there while I slept. In the same basement room in which
I slept on the futon Baby had his workbench, which con-
sisted of a desk he built out of plywood from the Rona and
a wall of tools and paintbrushes and a big plastic bin with
paint and varnish cans inside. This specific summer I am
remembering, he was building a chest for my mother to
keep her quilts in, and had just put a second coat of varnish
on it. I went to bed early that night, about six hours later,
and I remember lying in bed smelling the hot choking scent
of the varnish, thinking every few minutes that I had better
get up and go upstairs and ask my parents if it was okay
for me to be sleeping so near the chest while it was drying. But the heat and my uncharacteristically heavy fatigue
caused this thought to go in circles while I faded in and out
of sleep, and eventually slept through until morning. When
I awoke I had a very strong feeling that I am able to recall
to this day. Something about the varnish, something about

being so hot, a smell like hot pork, and a sensation between my legs that I would realize two years later was a sort of blip of orgasm. An accidental stimulation by squeezing my legs together around a pillow, or . . . something. I breathe in the smell of smoke, remember other moments, remember anything else.

The road recentres in my focus.

There is no parking space in front of the church so we circle the block, Baby lighting another cigarette. He hasn't a book with him so instead I pretend again to be the reporter from the big magazine.

"What made you decide to write a memoir now," I ask him, "and never before?"

"Not enough had happened," he says.

There is a tension in the car. He must know this irritates me. Some small part of him, buried deep, must remember what happened last time we played this game?

"I have begun to worry I will lose these moments if I don't write them down," he says.

"I see," I say, still in the reporter voice.

If only I could get them on the phone this instant. Prove that he is here, he is alive, listen to him. But, as things go, they will call when he is out, mentally, and I will make an excuse, or he will fumble his way through and if he is lucky the reporter will assume it is an issue of hearing loss, or of technological ignorance, and not an impending complete lack of awareness and identity. An inability to produce another work. For there is another work coming, and perhaps the most important one. I just need to get the facts straight, put the right words down in the right order, and get it onto the shelves before he reveals himself to be empty. People are becoming suspicious, as if it is their business. Mark Richman sending emails with a new curtness. All because Baby had some ideas that they liked, because he made them feel like he was their friend, because he got into their heads and disturbed them and now they feel they are owed something. Well, me too.

I ask him what he thinks about the contemporary literary scene in Canada. He says, "I don't," throws his cigarette on the road.

There's a spot a block or so away from the church and I worry about the image of myself and Baby approaching the building, a coping saw in his hand. But there are others. In fact, as we near the side entrance leading to the back where the rows of trees are growing, a handful of men are in view, all with saws. This is a scene I try to commit to memory. Try to shape into the beginning of something that maybe I will get to writing later. The men filed around back behind the church, saws in hand. Bad writing.

I feel certain that every year in my childhood my family brought home a spruce tree and twisted the tree holder's thick screws into its trunk. Baby, however, insisted that it was always pine. Pine, he said, is the classic. There was one year, in fact it was the same year as with the varnish in the basement by the futon, but in December of course, when Baby brought home a pine tree instead of a spruce. And this is when he began to insist it had always been a pine. I knew that this was untrue because I had never seen a pine tree in an indoor setting. Its long soft needles, like horse hair, were feminine and creepy to me. I had dreams of them stroking my face, my body, with a feeling that got twisted with feelings I had when my mother was unhappy with me. I began to form some sort of association between pine trees and my mother, spruce trees and my father. And so my father bringing home a pine and insisting that I had misremembered meant something else about my memory. Over time I become more and more unreliable.

Small young families walk in lineups through the paths between rows of trees. A mother and daughter— the mother seems ten years younger than I am—with no saw stop briefly at each tree, stroke the needles. The small daughter lifts her face to each one and inhales. I lose Baby in my observation of the mother and daughter. I'm thinking about my own mother. We too had small moments together, though in later years I discovered that my mother feels we never connected. In a journal entry (yes, I regret being so disrespectful as to open the journal) she once described me as "a stranger made from [her] own body." All along I'd seen her as the cold one, figured we had a special way of communicating with one another that existed primarily in the realm of the unspoken. In any case, it's too late to change that now. I don't know how to speak to her any other way. Whereas with Baby, due to his own changes, I am able to be flexible. I read him like the weather and I adapt. At times I am a mother, at times I am a machine that keeps things in order.

I do insist I didn't read the journals out of malice. It's just she left them in the house, and I wanted answers. *What really happened to Pauline* type thing. Okay, so after I've read the whole family's secrets, I face the consequences in what I find. Now I am burdened with the knowledge, and complacent in its evilness. If I'd never known, I might think myself some sort of angel.

Baby has chosen a tree when I catch up to him.

"A beautiful pine," he says, clasping the branch of a spruce in his hand.

Certainly he is testing me.

"It's a spruce, Dad," I say.

He plucks a needle off of the branch, holds it between his fingers. He tries to offer it to me and I won't take it. Really, I should, but at times I just cannot do what he wants me to.

"You are disrespecting me in front of all of these people!" he shouts.

He hasn't been like this with me, not in my adulthood. I'd almost forgotten this side of him.

"It's okay," I say.

The young girl from earlier is a couple trees over. She looks up at Baby, then at me. Her mother pulls her closer, moves away. I worry that she might have recognized Baby, seen that something is wrong with him.

The tree is lopsided, short. No sense trying to change his mind. He hands me the saw and it occurs to me that I've never used one. I crouch to dig the blade into the trunk but he wants us each to take one side of the handle. He crouches too, opposite me. For a moment he sways, then steadies himself with a bare hand in the snow. The skin over the back of his hand is thin and discoloured.

I take my end of the saw, guide it toward the tree against the resistance of Baby's grip, and dig the metal teeth into the bark. The bark is thick and waxy on the outside, and it's tougher to move the saw than I expected. We strain against the tree, pushing toward Baby and away from me.

The saw comes loose. Baby is thrown off of his feet, falls on his back, and a spruce branch from another tree scrapes across his face. He doesn't make a sound, and for a moment he appears unconscious. Then, his eyes tense. I worry someone nearby has seen everything and will accuse me of having hurt him. My self-consciousness freezes me, prevents me from offering anything to him. I take the saw from his hand, which causes him to open his eyes.

Baby has sat up. He is out of breath and something about him has changed since before he stumbled.

I feel aware of others watching now, as certainly we are causing some sort of scene. I begin to imagine the ways this can be misconstrued and a familiar sense of dread rises in me. At the very core of things nothing is wrong. Then why does it feel differently? Always, it does. The dark edges. But it can always be explained away. Always I take whatever hints of accusations I've begun to form and I eat them.

IN THE CAR WITH the tree bundled up in twine and tied over top, we don't say a word. Baby, although I am convinced he does not remember the events on the lot, seems to punish me with silence. When I speak to him he responds, "What?" Eventually I catch on and stop repeating myself.

Usually I take a route through town that runs behind the block where Baby's childhood home sits, surrounded by debris and with demolition permits in the downstairs

windows. But I am distracted, and I drive right past, realizing too late when I see that Baby's face is turned toward
the property, looking silently at the front half of the house,
through which one can see straight to the backyard, as the
back half has been torn off.

"Stop!" he shouts. His voice cracks and I am embarrassed by the error. Things like this do not happen in
books; a broken line gets rewritten. "Pull in," he says, "my
house."

"No, that's not where we live."

"I know that," he says with a hint of an edge. "My
home."

I realize I've talked down to him, assumed he's all the
way gone. He stares into the empty windows with an
expression of perfect understanding.

"I need to say goodbye," he says.

"To the house?" I say.

"I need to say goodbye to the house."

We took longer at the lot than expected. Now we are
meant to get to the bakery before it closes to pick up gifts
for the neighbours and for my mother and her husband.
Small jars of jam and preserves, cookie ingredients layered
in jars and ready to bake. I know that if I rush him he will
only feel more like a child, will act out against my laughable authority.

So, again I leave him, just as at Mark Richman's. More
and more I feel I fold his actions into mine. I will select the
gifts, address them, sign them with his name, mail them
out. It's not that I mind the small chore, but last year at this
time, things wouldn't have gone this way.

I make him promise me he will stay in the car, look out the passenger window at the house but not cause any sort of scene on the street. Well, I put it differently. He has his hands up on the glass like an animal in a cage. When I walk away from the car, I see his skin pressed flat against the window, the rest of him concealed by the glare of the sun hitting the glass.

THE WEATHER HAS REACHED a point of no return. The snow falls and stays, the short rises in temperature during which we remove a layer, walk with a certain freeness to our bodies, have ended. I move through the main strip of town; I am stalling. Later, after the call with the reporter, I will have a conversation with Baby that I do not want to have. At least, it will depend on his state. Perhaps he won't be there at all today. Sooner or later there will have to be someone else in the house, someone professional.

The cold air tightens the downtown. Doors are closed, whereas in summer stores seem to pour out the front doors to meet the bustle of the street. Snow freezes into little scooped-out corners in windowsills. Sometimes I think it must be hard on them, the buildings. But I'm thinking of my hands, my tingling cheeks, when I feel pity. Really it's about me, when the buildings themselves stand in noble indifference. I push myself into the wind and continue down the main street.

The bakery occupies the ground floor and basement of an old stone building. They are known in travel guides for their big fluffy cinnamon buns, baked in the basement,

and preserves in little bulbous jars. The workers behind
the counter are almost exclusively young high-school
and college-aged girls, often daughters of the owners or
kitchen staff or other business owners on the main strip.
Growing up I envied them. Of course, different girls.
Different daughters of different business owners. Once a
year we stayed in my father's childhood home with his
parents, sister, and brother-in-law. Sleeping in my father's
childhood bedroom made me feel as though he were there
with me, his child self. I felt that we had an understanding, myself and the child father, but not my father and his
past self. And so we kept secrets. I longed for that version
of him, rather than the one that I knew. Baby would walk
with me—just me, while Pauline stayed with my mother
and the extended family—to the bakery and take me into
the basement and let me pick out any one thing that I
wanted. Every year I would have the same gingerbread
cookie decorated like a little blonde woman in a pink dress.
They were dry, and decorated in big batches that meant
the details were off, sometimes an eye having a trail of
frosting connecting to the hair, or the red mouth smeared
into a frown. But I liked them. I think they reminded me
of the girls behind the counter. Unequivocally feminine.
Whereas I was awkward; for years I wore boys' clothing,
not because I liked it but because I felt there was something inherently brutish about me, and something that
would show even more by contrast if I were to try to
masquerade as something elegant, girlish. So somehow
desiring the garishly female cookie made me feel closer
to some semblance of womanhood. And closer to the

counter girls, as if in a way I was consuming them. More recently I go in and buy the drip coffee in a Styrofoam cup, sometimes a slice of banana bread with chocolate chips. Today, because I am stalling, I make the rounds. I want to give Baby enough time that we are able to go home without a fight.

Nothing piques my interest really. After a while it is all the same. Cedar-smelling votive candles, silk stockings, little stacked house-made marshmallows decorated to look like snowmen. It's dark down here. The whole place smells overwhelming, especially in the basement. A woman descends the stairs and I remember that I am not alone. I felt for a moment almost as if I were only inside in a memory, wherein other patrons could be added or subtracted as I filled in the details of the room. The woman stops at a display of boxed tea and I go back upstairs. Today I order just a coffee, leave the confections behind. They don't appear to make the gingerbread women anymore. And behind the counter is an older woman I recognize from other trips in, though who I have not established a rapport with. It is my own fear that makes me inaccessible.

I saw the demolition notice on Baby's childhood home months ago, and decided not to tell him. He did ask once to go and see it and I put it off, let him forget. When I envision the machines tearing the house down I imagine it is fully furnished with everything I remember from our stays as a family. However, a new family moved in after Baby's parents passed away, one year apart.

My memories of the layout of the house change, and really I only have small glimpses that I am unable to patch

together. The closet in the basement with a curtain instead
of a door, something strange and balloon-like hanging
from a hat rack, visible through the basement window
looking out at the backyard. A row of big stones sup-
porting the raised garden in the backyard—no, that's my
mother's garden, in our home. In the bathroom next to
Baby's childhood bedroom there was a doll, a human form
with a dog's face and a head of brown hair, and it had a
peculiar grease on it, sort of brownish around the edges
of facial features, and there was an overall shine. Perhaps
from so many years of condensation and splashing from
the shower and steam. But I felt afraid to get too near to
it, especially to touch it. And so I would go into the bathroom (it was the only bathroom on the upper floor, and I
did my best to avoid going down to the main floor where
I would surely run into someone, most likely my grandmother, who took a particular disliking to me, or so I felt,
and that feeling was supported by various acts of passive
aggression over a number of years, and a general lack of
warmth that one might expect from such an archetypal
figure) and close my eyes so as not to see the greasy anthro-
pomorphic dog propped up in the inner back corner of the
pink acrylic tub.

I once told Pauline, and now I can't recall if the story
is one that I invented or if it is in fact true, that I had
gone into the bakery on the main street and down in the
basement among the rows of gingerbread ladies and gingerbread men was a cookie decorated with a dog's face,
akin to the doll in the bathroom. In any case I looked for
one today and of course it was not there.

I am going to suggest to Baby that we hire some help, not because he is in need of more care than I am able to provide but because I am inadequate. That will be my angle. I need help so that I can work more, write him a wonderful book. It's not so untrue. It's just that I feel that things are happening, a little bit. Now that I am left alone with the book, no longer having to explain, to read him the passages and study his face for displeasure. Plus, there are certain behaviours of Baby's I would like to see handled by a professional. A couple times he has asked me to sleep in his room with him. Just in case something happens. To him? No, to me. He worries someone will break into the house and hurt me. "What," I asked him, "would you be able to do for me if they did?" Yes I could have been a little bit more compassionate. It's just I get my back up. And, see, the suggestion caused a spark of a memory in me. We did have a break-in once, in my childhood. Somebody mostly harmless, drunk, convinced he was in his own house. Baby diffused the situation, sent him home in a taxi, but that night he slept in Pauline's bedroom with her. My mother slept in mine with me. But that's all. Otherwise Baby slept in the master bedroom and my mother slept with him or with me, except once or twice I had a friend stay over and we would sleep back to back, assuring each other through our posture that we were sharing out of necessity and not interest. Or perhaps I was projecting. I didn't necessarily know how to be around other girls, other than my sister. It wasn't until I was in the second or third grade that I was allowed to go to a friend's house after school on my own. Before that, my mother would come with me. Though I don't think it was on her own terms. Baby didn't like me to be out of my mother's sight, even though he himself was often absent. And so it was an event the first time I went to a sleepover with five friends, and we stayed up all night watching movies and eating popcorn popped by the one girl's mother and I felt something I'd never felt before and all I knew was that that was how I wanted to feel for the rest of my life. One of them. A real girl, with a beginning and an end, and not a quiet audience to adult instability. Of course, that's how I see it now. Back then, all I knew was that I was not normal.

Baby circled the block in his car, over and over, all night long, waiting for the house to catch fire, waiting to come in and save me from burning to death with five other girls. He didn't tell me for years. And when he did, I said, "What about the others?"

One day this week I will have to call my mother and confirm about Christmas, ask if I am able to bring Baby, insist he will behave. Anyway, she is much easier on him now after settling in with her husband, and his children right down the street. I guess I haven't mentioned the strange thing? It's her first husband she is married to at present. They divorced for thirty-two years, during which time he married another woman and raised three children, while my mother married my father and raised us, and then in their sixties he and my mother remarried. So there is a rightness about all of it (on paper) that predates me, that seems to take away from things that happened in the thirty-two-year window. As if Pauline, Baby, and me are part of some detour and now she has corrected. This is what I was saying about my twenties, too. Oh but I don't mean to play the victim. It's not as if I felt that way before I did a little after-the-fact analysis, trying to dig up some explanation for . . . everything. It's just easier this way, viewing myself as a blip in an otherwise steady life. If I can't have it, my mother can. I'm romanticizing. I must be bored. So I will give her a call.

I've lost track of time, and other customers have moved past me as if I am a fixture in the store. As if on cue, the cash register bell rings like a phone call and I am waved forward. A small tea light burns in a reindeer-shaped votive holder on the counter. My memory of the sleepover prompts me to imagine the store on fire.

WHEN I RETURN WITH two cups of coffee, a paper bag of gingersnaps, some small decorative gifts, Baby is no longer in the car. I panic, store the bags in the backseat and imagine I'll never find him, dumbly, when I look up and see he is on the front porch of the house. He is knocking and knocking on the door, which has to its immediate left a jagged hole of missing bricks with a view through to the backyard.

The openness of the structure appears like a dollhouse. I imagine giant hazy figures, Baby's parents, playing with the house's innards, moving objects around, picking up small figurine versions of Baby and myself and Pauline and my mother and throwing them around, crushing us under their feet. I imagine them locking up Baby in a room, placing Pauline somewhere safe in the grass outside.

I go and retrieve him, turn away so he does not know I've thought twice about what he was doing up there. He has returned to subservience, takes my elbow on our way back to the car. I almost feel nostalgic for when he was arguing with me about the trees. At least then he was my father again.

I AM TASKED WITH setting up the tree while Baby takes his call into his office. He was upset with me when we arrived home, and I don't know if it was because of the tree or the house, but he refused my help with the interview. From the living room I can hear the soft even pacing of his voice. He seems okay.

In the end the tree fits where he insisted it has always gone. Surely he can't have been right. It was always near the entryway? With clumsy ambition I dragged the thing up the front steps and into the corner of the living room where the ceiling slants down under the staircase, left a trail of needles on the carpet. Now, grinding the metal posts of the tree stand into its bark, my head hurts. I feel a peculiar excitement at the thought of showing Baby that I've gotten it up.

Around its base I lay down a quilted skirt, wrap a beaded garland in big loose loops, place all of our precious mismatched bulbs on branches one by one. In the box of ornaments there is a broken angel with a face that resembles Pauline's. Well, it doesn't so much, when I think about it. But we've always as a family called it "Angel Pauline."

I wonder now if this suggested to her that being just "Pauline" was markedly inferior.

Baby comes out of his office and is pleased, wants to sit and look at the tree while he drinks his coffee. I made a pot of decaf after dinner, already I need to start another one. He asks me to keep the lights on the setting where they change their flickering pattern every thirty seconds or so. I wonder if otherwise he might forget what he is looking at.

I perform small tasks around the main floor of the house, make more coffee, drink more coffee, and each time I pass Baby he is looking at the tree, and crying.

CHILDREN
By Baby Davidson

Chapter I

I was early to live in guilt. I adopted the heavy posture of an older man in my teens, heavier yet in my twenties.

I saw men drop their shoulders under the weight of extramarital affairs, of lying, gambling, and stealing. They aged into it like thick noble trees reaching the end of a great and natural cycle. I saw large and notable deals end in life-shattering losses. Fifty years stretch out the seams of a starched suit. Men begrudge the body that holds them back, that causes them pain when they do what they have always done. The mind becomes a prisoner in a slow degrading machine. Then the mind goes. They say a man becomes a man when he loses his father, but what does he become when he loses himself?

At fifteen years old I ruined my life. Perhaps it was after having observed this slow slouching toward death in my forefathers that I came to achieve a certain air of disillusion. I did not believe in sin, not in the way I was instructed. Perhaps I am beginning too late. How about this:

At seven years old I stood in the hallway coat closet, eyes closed, and whispered, "There is no God." I needn't tell you not a thing happened in that instant. The world continued to rotate at its same pace; the weather moved in predictable patterns broadcast by attractive men and women in formal wear; my body remained upright, inhaled, exhaled.

By this I illustrate my disbelief in sin, hell, father, son, ghost.

No other memorable events occurred on that day. By this I mean to say the Godfearing docility was short-lived.

This is not a story about God or about losing Him.

It was as I said at fifteen that I began to lose control of my impulses. I acted in ways that at first surprised me, then began to bring on a familiar feeling of dread. I walked for long stretches of time, alone and in distress. I walked in the opposite direction of the girls who stood streetside in big-haired bunches and whistled at anyone who walked by. And yet often it was me they whistled at. I always ended up back in their domain, as if the city were one big racetrack. Every time prior I'd delighted in the attention, stayed a moment too long, but turned back home to stutter over an excuse as to my whereabouts, making a promise to myself I'd not venture there again. It was as easy as anything the day I offered the thirty dollars of my allowance for a blowjob in the bathroom of the Main Street YMCA. All the way home, with my penis feeling like a foreign object in my pants, I couldn't help but keep thinking, *It was just like paying for any old item in a store*. The woman was tall, slender, flat-chested, good-humoured. I remember thinking for an instant we might develop a friendship.

But the guilt grew inside of me like cancer, starting at my repulsive boyhood. I paid for more, and more often. Different women, always different women. I pleasured myself to thoughts of my teachers, to my mother's churchgoing friends. There were times I missed out on something—a game, a party, an appointment—because I was in the bathroom, or my bedroom, waiting with fitful impatience for the end of the stretch of time I would have to wait between one orgasm and the next. How had I

reduced my life to this, I wondered. I felt its absence in everything. An indulgent meal, a weekend morning sleep-in, a hot
bath, nothing gave anything close to the satisfaction.

This and other shameful recollections had been keeping me
awake in the Manhattan hotel suite. Though I had matured, lost
some of the edge on my self-sorryness, things never shifted back
to how they'd been before. I'd learned to live with the guilt, with
the dissatisfaction in all things that didn't end in orgasm. But
The Business seemed to offer just that. The *deal!* The *advance!*
New York!!!

I'd not felt that old familiar guilt for the bigger part of the
night. I'd felt engaged with each passing moment. So much so
that the night slipped through my fingers like water. I talked
about this and that with a number of industry so-and-sos. It
was my first major publication, and my first major advance.
Six months out from the second installment, I blew the first one
on dates with Catherine. She charged me next to nothing, but I
couldn't get enough of her.

An offer was floated, for me to sign with an American
agency. I don't remember what I'd later say, though I didn't end
up signing. A dormant hunger had been awakened. I'd begun to
feel irreverent, resentful. I told men to their faces I couldn't care
less about their synopses, their elevator pitches. I let my eyes
glaze over when young publicists told me of their trajectories.
There, accompanied by the two students, both of whom I hoped
to bed, I felt a familiar tingle of desire, a need to be somewhere
else, to be accomplishing something. If I couldn't have sex, I at
least needed to be writing.

Though I didn't know it at the time, this was just one example of how the book tours would routinely go. The particular

gaiety was due to it being my first, but otherwise, they bleed together in my memory, like a too-long vacation. In my recollection I am always leaving, or hoping to leave. They are but a waste of time.

Making contact at the hand, hearing a name I'd soon forget, moving on. Always, and quickly, my ego would be poisoned with guilt. My crotch would lead me upstairs, or into a cab, or into a hotel bathroom.

The girls had hovered nervously, coaching one another about approaching recognizable figures. I'd felt they were a burden, suddenly, and wanted to make use of them. I was embarrassed by their eagerness to be in that room, as if that room had offered them some sort of window into their futures. Was that not why I'd brought them, anyway?

In the hotel suite, one of them had begun to cry. "Is this why you've brought us here?" she'd asked, with a cruel expression about her face I imagined she'd adopted from her mother. I was undressed, on my back on the bed.

I'd mistakenly assumed they'd been waiting for my advance, the both of them. They left in a huff, holding hands, a force to be reckoned with.

This and a series of repulsive moments from my youth prevented my mind from quieting, my eyes shutting. The great futuristic lights of New York City were superimposed onto the ceiling, and the backs of my eyelids.

Frantically, I packed my things. I felt a fool for having seen myself as some sort of impressive figure. The book, the money, it was ill-fitting and destined to fail. I felt I only had to wait until someone realized the cheapness of my tricks. I was a young idiot, driven by stupid primal desire. I had no grip on the arts.

There were seats left on the next flight to Toronto. I felt disoriented by the white fluorescent light of the airport, the fresh-faced receptionist. I considered for a moment the cost of having her.

The flight was smooth and ominous. I kept anticipating some turbulence. Surely I couldn't be alone in my terror; I couldn't carry it with me and not somehow have an effect on the suspended structure. When the stewardess had passed one way and back with her cart of drinks and packets of chips, I unbuckled and pulled my way back to the bathroom to relieve myself.

Returning to my car, I felt a great sense of failure. I drove with the same smoothness of the flight from New York, passing alike houses on alike streets, considering how I might go about ending my—

10

—OH, I CANNOT HELP but embellish. No, that was not the night he left my mother. It's just sometimes a symbol is truer than the fact. *Children*, I've called it, after his poem, and for our absence in the story. Where are we to be found in his notes? Anyway it is bad writing. I highlight the phrase, "by this I mean to say," press delete, and go downstairs.

IN THE KITCHEN, I tidy up. I fold a stack of take-out menus from the top of the fridge and put them in the recycling. We never ordered from them, anyway. I started to collect them when I moved in, feeling I might live with more abandon than I had in the city, where the pressures of younger, more driven women made me guilty about my meals. But, whatever self-consciousness I lost took the gratification with it. Most times eating feels to be just another task to complete, to move swiftly through the day.

There are multiple phone numbers on the back of the memory loss pamphlet from the pharmacy; there's one for an emergency helpline, one for counselling and therapy, and one for home nurse services. When I call the home nurse number I am told I am fourth in line, and the receptionist's voice is cut by a tone and replaced by classical piano.

Catherine. Baby answered the door as if he could feel her there, now they stand chatting in the entryway just out of ear shot. It's not that I think they are saying anything of note, but still I catch myself straining to listen over the hold music. There is something about her; he loves her, I think.

When they move into the living room, I take the cordless phone out with me to get the newspaper so they don't hear me. The cold outside is bright and refreshing, and I feel like I could stand outside all day. My mind is changed when a chill runs through me with a gust of wind. Plus if they notice I'm out here, well that's not much better than if they overhear me. The hold music cuts, and a voice that sounds very far away says, "Hello?"

Another time. I hang up, go back inside.

In the newspaper's entertainment section, a big picture of Baby. It's a black-and-white photograph, which I recognize as having been taken by my mother. There's something about the way his face is that tells me she was behind the camera. The headline: PORTRAIT OF THE ARTIST AS AN OLD MAN.

Quickly I am running out of time to finish the book. The reporter from the literary magazine called me earlier to fact-check some of what Baby said, described parts of

WHAT WE BOTH KNOW

the interview as "stilted, at times nonsensical." Catherine comes to me in the kitchen. Her presence in the house satisfies Baby, who is now in his armchair in front of the TV. However, he's watching the news and not his usual show. Perhaps he's embarrassed in front of Catherine.

"I thought of something," she says to me, quietly. She smells different. Nice, but more synthetic than normal. Did she put something on in anticipation of seeing Baby? I feel a twinge of something: Why would she?

I turn over the newspaper so she can't see the article about Baby.

"I need help with the dogs," she says. "If you come help me out, you can work off what you need for the car." She mouths the words "the car," as if Baby might overhear. As if he might understand even if he did overhear. I have seen him look at the vehicle a number of times without noticing the damage, or if he did notice he paid no mind to it. In any case, I feel compelled to take the opportunity to be closer to Catherine. There is something about her, or, something about how I feel when I am near her. She is like home. But Baby? He wouldn't have anybody in the hours I would be at Catherine's. Surely I can't.

I ask her if I can get back to her. I feel overtaken by emotion at the thought of somebody thinking of me. That Catherine, on her own time, came up with a way to help me. Plus, I don't know how otherwise I'd afford to fix the damage. I feel I can't get a quote, even, until I come with a good story for how it happened.

She grins. "Get back to me." Her teeth are yellow in a way that I like, because it reminds me of coffee and cigarettes and red wine, and those things are the things a person likes when they know how to enjoy life.

CATHERINE AGREED TO STAY the afternoon with Baby, which means I have time to drive into the city. There are boxes in Pauline's apartment that her roommate packed up and left outside the unit door. She said she would rather not see me, and no hard feelings, but it would be too emotional for her. Plus somebody else lives in the room now, and they haven't been told about what happened. I can't help but feel that she is angry. I don't blame her; I've left the things with her for over a year now, not wanting to go into the apartment again. When I went in during the first few days after the incident, none of it was real yet. I kept looking over my shoulder expecting to see Pauline walk into the room and throw herself on her bed. Her bed, the last place she ever was to have an idea, a memory, a breath.

On my way I try again with the home nurse line. Describing Baby out loud feels like I am defaming him. Somebody is available this week for a consultation, they say, and I want to hang up again. How am I to ease him into the idea in under a week? But, I am nearing the apartment building and want to get off the line, so I agree, and consider calling back later to cancel.

As I near the building I feel lighter in my seat. A few more blocks and I may not even be able to press the gas pedal. I pull off of the main street and onto the side road where her building is, and her roommate is out on the balcony digging around in a planter. She is wearing a red button-up dress and a straw hat, and looks out of place so near the city's downtown core. I get out of the Jeep and when I shut my door she looks up, waves. So, we will pretend we did not agree not to see each other. I wave back.

The furniture in the apartment has been rearranged. I am relieved when the roommate does not offer to show me around, instead hovers by the doorway with the boxes at her feet.

"I'm sorry I didn't come earlier," I say. I stack the boxes so that I may be able to carry both down to my car in one trip, and not have to come back into the apartment again. They are light, probably filled with clothes.

"You look like her," says Meaghan.

"Thank you," I say, and carry the boxes down the stairs as quickly as I can, and load them into my car, and drive two blocks and park and begin to cry.

WHEN I RETURN HOME, Baby is reading by the window. Catherine has just left. I feel a pang of hurt, as if she has left specifically in order not to see me. No, I remember, she has thoughts independent of me. There is a knock at the front door and I figure she must be back. Maybe forgot something, or saw my car pull in as she was leaving. What it is exactly that I want from her, I still haven't determined.

When I think of her I am distracted by a conversation we had a few nights ago, at her place. I didn't tell her anything, nothing specific, but I guess in one way or another she understood what was on my mind: Pauline.

"You were always such a happy kid," she'd said. She'd
said it as if by saying it she had the power to make it true.
Or, maybe it was true, and wasn't that worse? I hoarded
it, and turned away when I didn't like what I saw. In a way
I'd willed myself to forget that Catherine had witnessed so
much of me, before I gained the steady control of adulthood. I felt a twinge of shame at the thought of the breadth
of her experience of me. Whereas I've only seen her as she
is, complete.

"Really?" I'd asked her, and she'd smiled.

It's not Catherine at the door but Mark Richman with
a bottle of wine, and his wife. They seem to crowd into the
doorway, taking up more space than any other two people.
It is as if they can see from the entrance the house in its
entirety. All of its flaws, everything needing to be put away,
the dust along the tops of shelves. I have to wonder if Mark
has seen the headline and that is the reason behind the surprise visit. Perhaps he is sniffing things out for himself.

The wine he's brought is homemade, with a photograph
of him and his wife on the label. In frilly white cursive it
says *Happy Holidays!*

I lead them in, bring four glasses to the table. Baby sees
Mark's wife first, and doesn't seem to recognize her. Then
he sees Mark, lights up. His posture stiffens into something
proud, businesslike. The men shake hands.

"Hey, Mark," says Baby in a new voice, different than
the one he uses with me.

The three of them sit around the kitchen table and I
make do with what we have in the fridge. I arrange sliced
deli meats, cheeses, cracked wheat crackers, sweet pickles,

WHAT WE BOTH KNOW   121

squares of dark chocolate on a wooden cutting board. Defrost some frozen sliced sourdough in the toaster oven.

Mark is telling Baby about whose books are coming out when, how big some of the advances are, how small others are. Baby nods along, maybe understands. Mark's wife says "Thank you" each time I place something on the table. Her presence makes me miss Catherine, like any other woman will not do. The men, well they're off in their own world.

When I join them, the table closes in. I feel all of their eyes on me. Mark's wife seems to have been waiting for me, and once they're all looking at me she says, "Are you writing, Hillary?"

"Here and there," I say. "I'm not so good."

"I'm sure that's not true," she says.

Mark grins at me, says nothing. He produces an envelope from his bag, which he has resting against his chair. The bag, since he arrived, has been a sort of Chekhovian gun.

"Marcus," he says to Baby. "An old friend of yours has reached out. I thought this letter might be of interest to you."

Mark's wife smiles at me.

Baby's hands tremble as he opens the envelope. I realize this is how it's been for quite some time, but I've never thought consciously of the tremor. It all seems to go at once. I try not to look too closely or I'll see that his skin is falling off of him, his eyes have no shine. He reads, slowly, nods, and gives the envelope back to Mark.

"No," he says.

"Baby," says Mark. "Think about it."

"They're mocking me. They think I've gone senile." With one hand he gestures to the letter and the other, I can see, is clenched.

The Arthurs have reached out to invite Baby to a literary gala in Toronto in three weeks, Mark's wife says to the table, and they're awarding him the honour of Most Influential Ontario Writer. They've created the award for Baby, it will be the first one, and they also want to invite him back into the Arthurs. "How wonderful," she says, looking at me. As if I might convince him.

A lull in his career, and now they are reuniting. They include Baby in the reunion, employ a certain professional tone that avoids specifics, suggests he never was not one of them. I do understand why he is resistant. But to me, the Arthurs seem like celebrities or like gods, as I have never met them. They have always been presented as part of the past, eternalized as something perfect, precious, but evil. I feel a new excitement about the potential of this future for Baby, reaching back, reconnecting. Maybe he will even remember. Maybe this can all go in the book.

"You know," Mark's wife says to me. She still has not been introduced to me, and at this point she probably will not be. "I held you as a baby."

And Pauline, too, I wonder?

I had this naive hope when I was in Mark's office that he had forgotten me, and that the years to him have been the same as they've been to me. Though to me what has been a passage from childhood into my teens and then into adulthood, very separate and distinct eras, has to Mark just been a length of time in middle age. He had the same awareness in my early years as he does now. Suddenly I am embarrassed to have spoken to him coolly, like I am somebody new.

ONE OF MY EARLIEST memories of the literary world, perhaps at four or five years old, is a holiday party hosted by Mark and his literary agency. They'd rented an event hall and catered with small quartered sandwiches with spreads and meats I'd never seen before, and drinks on silver trays, and a tree so tall it nearly touched the sloping ceiling, higher than our house, and around the bottom of the tree were gifts wrapped all in the same gold foil. I begged Baby to give the charity donation that would be rewarded with one of the mystery gifts, and he had, for myself and Pauline. When I remember the party I forget about Pauline until this moment, when I remember the gifts. I forget my mother too, who is described in this scene in one of Baby's books, but not in my memory of the evening. In fact much of the description of this particular evening, in his book, contradicts my memory. Under the tree there were gifts labelled *girl* and gifts labelled *boy* and all but one of the girl gifts were claimed and so Pauline was given a boy gift and I was given a girl gift. This is where I don't remember anything else, for in my memory there is a certain darkness to the party and then we are home, as if in a dream in which the brain doesn't fill in the information about what is inside each or any of the wrapped gifts and so instead ends the scene or switches to something else entirely. But, as Baby wrote in the book, Pauline's gift actually ended up being a book of Baby's—lots of the boy gifts were books written by the agency's talent. My gift was a plastic baby doll that could be filled with water through the mouth and that would then urinate through an opening between the legs. At the sight of this, he says, I began to cry, and cried until Baby took me home and hid the doll somewhere I would not encounter it again until my teens, at which point I would be overcome with a very strange physical sensation and immediately return it to its hiding spot. I don't remember where it is that I found it, and now it occurs to me I might come across it again soon.

The book with that scene, the holiday party, is called *King of the Whole Wide World*. Baby referred to it in an interview with the *Toronto Star* as a portrait of a failed father, and an attempt at redemption. Setting fire to himself before anyone else could do it. Proving that he is bigger than his past, and in this way relieving himself of responsibility. Yes, he understands. In fact, he understands better than anyone else. I asked him once, in more lucid times, what exactly he meant by failure, "I mean, precisely, which moments," and he said, "Sometimes we say things for the sake of an interesting interview."

Now I remember my mother. I remember the doll too. My mother had tried to persuade me to think of it differently. Whereas Baby had hidden it away in agreeance, my mother had wanted me to care for the object. After all, it was a gift. But I was not of her kind. It wasn't until adulthood that I began to side with my mother, and even then not as often as she would like.

Pauline never read the novel. I don't think she read much of Baby's work, or at least not as much as I did. She too tried to coerce me into settling down that day. When we got back to the house I'd gone into my room, shut the door. Pauline tapped quietly with her nails, opened the door a crack, and pressed her face between the door and its frame. It was exactly what I wanted, for her to come placate me. The feeling lifted, but I was a stubborn child and too embarrassed to have a shift in mood in front of her. And so I pushed on the door, squeezing the sides of her face, and she'd called me an asshole and gone back downstairs to our parents. In my bedroom I felt outcast from the family. Misunderstood, unable to come around like the others. This, of course, predated the role reversal. When things got bad for Pauline, when a darkness was cast over her teenage years, I became the more accessible of the two. I became the middleman for communication with her, listened when they called her lazy, selfish, unforgiving.

WHEN THINGS BEGIN TO wind down around the kitchen table I am able to slip out into the garage. The three of them have been quieted by the wine, now sit in near silence around the table, smiling politely, picking at scraps of food. I imagine my mother seeing Baby with a drink, how she would blame me for losing control of him. The car accident, the alcohol, nothing to show for myself with my own writing. Surely it can't look good.

In the first of Pauline's boxes, which I open with the jagged edge of the garage key, there is a pile of neatly

folded clothing. On the top is a pink silk slip with clusters
of white hydrangeas. I lay it across my lap, pet the material.

I remember the flowers, but not the garment. Blooming
bunches with curling green leaves. In trying to place the
slip in my memory, in trying to place Pauline in the slip,
trying to see her against the backdrop of a specific room,
in a specific apartment, at a specific time, I worry I am
rewriting. I worry I am muddying everything up, forgetting even more, tangling threads. Now I see her so clearly,
draped in the fabric, pulling at my arms to loosen me up. I
couldn't, or wouldn't, dance with her. Something old and
beloved on the radio in the living room. She was visiting
from her first year away at university. That's it! Our parents
were out—they were never out—and she'd tried to arrange
something mischievous in their absence but there was a
power outage and everyone was put out, so no one was
available to come over. In secret I was thrilled that she'd
have to resort to just me. Where had our parents gone? We
were in the final hour of daylight, and through the front
windows we could see neighbours tinkering with genera-
tors outside, standing in groups chatting, or knocking on
doors and borrowing tools and pieces of equipment. She
was jumping, landing each time with both feet pointing
one way, then the other, jostling my arms to try to get me
to move, laughing with her mouth wide open. "You're so
stiff!" she laughed. I meditate on the image for a moment,
hoping I've got it right.

Movement catches my eye. A small reddish bug crawls
across a pair of folded denim cut-offs. Something inside of
me jolts awake. I stand up and drop the slip out of my lap

and back away. I feel coated in insects, suddenly afraid of the idea of Pauline. As if I have encountered her corpse, being slowly consumed by the earth.

I can't leave things like this. Imagine if Baby were to come into the garage and find Pauline's clothes all strewn about the cement floor. Not to mention I don't want him seeing them at all. If I could I would enter into his brain, use fine tools to remove each memory of Pauline individually.

In my mind, back then, his fascination with Pauline boiled down to some secret sexuality in her person, or rather, a sexlessness in myself. For even as a child I was wise enough to know that a father shouldn't act as ours did. So, it was a flaw in me, rather than exclusively an exceptionality in Pauline, that led to our differing treatments. But when I saw other fathers with other daughters, something inside of me knew that none of it was right.

I am shaking when I approach the box again. Really, I almost laugh out loud at myself. I pick up the articles one by one, drop them into the box, and place the other, sealed box on top to hold the flaps shut. The slip is still on the floor where I left it. Carefully I inspect it, inside and out, for any trace of bugs. Nothing. I ball it up and enter the house through the garage's internal door, where I can stash the slip in the coat closet, and come back for it when the couple go home and Baby has gone to bed.

II

THIS MORNING I WOKE up with an itchy pink bite on my thigh. In a half-asleep state I ran my fingernails over it and a shudder shook through my body. A realness began to piece itself together as I went about my morning. I made my coffee, washed my face with cold water in the kitchen sink. Baby was in the bathroom listening to the radio loud while he showered.

Now, the television is on. He is in the reclining chair not paying much attention. I gather he likes the movement, the faint sounds, as something about the screen seems never to be lost on him. He is able to orient himself in the act of watching TV faster than inside the idea of being in his living room, in his house.

The dinner dishes from last night are on the kitchen counter. I use a fork to scrape the leftover food scraps into the trash under the sink, run some water into the wine glasses stained with little jewels of red in their bowls. I make up a plate with what's in the fridge—some hard cheeses, sliced salametti, some green grapes, big pitted olives in brine—and take the plate into Baby's office to get to work.

Looking through what I have in this section, I realize there is no mention of Pauline. Similarly, in his notes, nothing. Well, okay, there is one:

Hike and lunch, girls enjoying walking up ahead. Parents out of style.

I try to recall a scene, Baby and Pauline. Something he would record, how he would paint her in the memoir. I am filled with a familiar eerie feeling. The way he smiled when he looked over her schoolwork. The gifts he gave her for her birthdays and Christmas, always jewellery while for me it was, for example, a record player, a leather notebook. So, he knew enough not to write her down. He must, then, have struggled with his own behaviour. Or I'm projecting understanding onto him. Perhaps he just didn't consider any of it to be of note.

The air is thick with morning. I feel slow, infinitely far from the work. I try to go back, remember Pauline breathing, from the inside, her lungs, then from the outside, the little rise and fall of her chest through her blouse, and I can't. I start to pick her apart. A network, a machine, emotionless, perspectiveless. In this way I am artless in my fascination with repetition. I never can just leave something alone. In all of my memories now she dies. Different moments, different deaths. I write and erase. The writing feels like thumb twiddling, and I never get too far down the page. I try to work her into the existing scenes and it cheapens her. She becomes a focal point, a damsel. When I try to sit her on the sidelines, all eyes turn to her.

I search further through his notebooks. Finally there is one other mention:

*Told P not to drive in car with Jean's kid, too old.
Mistake?
H and Connie learned new recipe from book. Quite
a feast.*

The entry ends, and it's the final one in the journal. Then, I am left with nothing. No more scraps, no more stories. The rest is for me to fill in with what I know.

Instead, I go back to the beginning. I've yet to fill in the first few pages, where it all started. The details of Baby's adoption are few and mostly from memory, from what he told me in childhood. I've got his birth certificate, the information from the DNA site that trickles in and mostly tells us nothing. Nothing back from the niece and second cousin thus far. I called every high school in the district where his biological mother grew up and not one of them had a record of her name. It's as if Baby and his whole biological family exist outside of time.

The bite on my thigh nags at me. I dig into it with my fingernail until I can't stand the pain anymore. That should at least give me a rest from the itching for the time being. How could I forget? I rush to snatch the slip from the hall closet and take it back out to the garage where I hang it from a rubber-coated hook on the wall.

Back in. This time I cannot forget, or Baby will end up seeing. I can hardly even think about him going out there, touching the fabric. It repulses me.

On my way past I see his posture has changed; he's actually watching now. A newscaster speaks in that perfect unaffected way, delivers some tragedy.

"Hey," I say.

"Yes." He is consumed by the screen.

"Do you know if there are any more documents that might have information about your biological family?"

"What's that?" he says.

"Is there any more information?"

"Information," he repeats.

"Is there more about the adoption?"

"The adoption, yes." He gets up from his chair and looks back at the TV, as if to make sure it is still going to play in his absence, that it hasn't been switched off by his leaving the chair.

There is a filing cabinet next to Baby's big executive desk with a dent in its top drawer which makes it impossible to open, even when unlocked. Or so I've assumed, that is. Baby uses a pen from his desk drawer to put pressure on one corner, and pries the drawer open. I used to look through the cabinet in childhood, would snoop inside to look at old notes written between my parents, flick through pages and pages of documents that meant nothing to me.

Baby pulls out a haphazard stack of papers and puts them on the desk next to my computer. I really should tell him today about the family members found through the DNA site. Even now, though, I worry he'll lose his focus at any moment. He is nervously arranging the papers into a neater pile. Surely there will be something in here, some help forming a narrative I can use as the spine of the memoir. A name, a place, anything to find someone, anyone who knew Baby's biological family. I'd envisioned the hunt for his mother being the main plot, but it simply won't do if we don't make any headway in real life. If I can solve it myself, give him the answers he's been looking for his whole life, and in the book! Upon reading it he would find it solves everything. He would like that, surely.

In the folder with all of the adoption documentation are old phone bills, alumni magazines from the university, other things he has misplaced. It is all organized by date. The orderliness of the rest of the cabinet is beginning to fall apart more and more. It is as if each time he enters his office, he commits one destructive act.

There are pictures I drew as a child, a Polaroid photograph of myself and Pauline standing in front of the Big Apple on the side of the highway.

—

FUNNILY, WE RETURNED TO the apple in our teens, on a road trip from Toronto to Kingston. Pauline and I were visiting Queen's University (I must have just gotten my licence; she was barely twenty when she entered her degree) and we stopped at the Big Apple, having passed it with our parents on a number of occasions and considered it an outrageous whim to actually turn off the road and actually go into the thing again. There was a whole branded building behind the big wooden apple structure which must have been at least forty feet tall, the apple, and in the building they sold pies and cider and other merchandise, or so it can be assumed, as we did not go in this time or in childhood. Entrance to the apple was free and through a door down a pathway in the structure's exterior that opened to a staircase leading up to the top where there was a lookout. No one else was around that day in late August, at least not outside, and Pauline smoked cigarettes up at the top of the apple and tried to get me to smoke one but I was nervous I would cough and make things worse than if I just turned one down. I must have been turning seventeen. And I know the time because I know all things as being on one side or the other of the divide that is not yet having had sex, and having had sex, and the having happened in my seventeenth year, and that day on the lookout atop the big apple structure in Colborne, Ontario, I had not yet had sex. At that time I was actively fearing it, especially around Pauline who seemed to glow with her sexuality at all times. It was in the way she held her body, her earrings, her expensive perfume samples. She was wide-hipped and draped fabrics over her frame with an abandon that revealed a shade of comfort I couldn't imagine for myself. As if she were unfamiliar with the concept of sexlessness. I felt deep inside of myself that I simply would never be able to do it. We looked down at the road we'd been on and that we'd be rejoining to drive to the university and I felt a sense of freedom about the whole thing. It wasn't my life, my school, my car. I felt as though I was getting a preview into something that wasn't available to me yet. That maybe I would be able to prepare for when it was all mine. Do it even better, maybe. At the top of the apple in our denim cut-off shorts, and I don't quite remember if it was that I'd copied hers or it'd been a coincidence, Pauline put her arm around my shoulders and kissed me on the cheek and I felt something that shook me and that I never revisited again.

—

WHEN I THINK BACK to times I was with Pauline it feels as if I must have been alone. I remember the apple, the drive, the light rain when we arrived in Kingston, and the droves of logo-sweatered bodies moving into the castle-looking buildings. It was only me, I feel certain. Pauline, just as she is now, was only a ghost.

I recognize so many of the files in the cabinet the way I might recognize a face. So many papers passed over Baby's desk, and it didn't occur to me to read them. In childhood I saw the printed page as if it were an illustration, meaning no more than it appeared to at first glance.

Baby places documents in one stack, everything else in another. The top page now, while he sorts through some five-by-seven photographs, is a Second-Parent Adoption paper. Something from Baby's parents, I assume. That might have something! I read the text quickly so as not to give it any special attention. The real work cannot begin until he leaves the room, when I am left alone with his life and the document where I am writing it down.

Printed on the adoption form, in my mother's shaky block letters, is *PAULINE NOVAK*, with signatures from herself and Baby. A third signature that I cannot parse. Then he places a page atop that one and I cannot see any more of it. The new page is a bad photocopy of a vaccine chart.

Novak?

Then another page on top. A legal name change certificate dated 10 February 1983, when Pauline was given the surname Greene.

Novak?

My mother's first husband.

Baby holds a photograph out to me. "Look," he says. He is smiling. In the picture, my mother is sitting on a dock with her legs out in front of her, and they look so long, like a doll's. She is wearing a yellow one-piece swimsuit and looking into the camera grinning in this way. Me, Pauline, my mother, we all make that face, when we are truly happy. Our teachers would comment in school.

I feel sick to my stomach. Pauline Novak? And what about me? Am I a Novak, too? Well, he has reached the end of the pile of documents. There is no paper with my name on it. No name change form, no previous surname. In fact, I have seen pictures of the hospital room in which I was born. Baby leaning over the bed with his arm around my mother. I feel suddenly like a child spying on my parents from the top of the staircase, one ear pressed between the railing bars.

So, she is my mother's. And I am my mother's. But.

"Anyway," says Baby.

"Yeah," I say. I feel as if I might be sick. "Thanks, I'll get back to work."

He hovers for a moment and I worry he might stay. Then, he takes himself out of the room.

I am his. Only I am his. Pauline, for not being his, was punished. Sacrificed. Finally my sick, lifelong question has been answered. I feel ill with it, feverish. I feel that I am inside of Pauline in a way that both violates her and validates me. Holding her secrets, I feel closer to her, though they were not given to me, and so simultaneously there is a great irreparable distance. Not without cruelty, I feel some of my wounds healed by this information. The invisibility of my body to my father. The special effort to please Pauline, by my mother. The unrelenting presence of the first husband. My head is reeling. Did she know? Let her have known. But, oh, let her not have known.

How many times have I wished him dead, for what he did to her? What luck that there is nothing out there listening, no reward for prayer. For now I'd like to hook him up to some network of tubes and monitors and syringes, replace his body over time with new mechanical parts, upload his brain until he is all computer, anything to keep him alive, anything to ensure that he never again will be in the same place as Pauline.

I search "Pauline" in his emails. My hands are trembling. There are dozens from family members and industry professionals offering condolences. One from my mother asking, curtly, for something to be mailed to her. There is one from Daniel, with the subject: "A Proposal." In it he asks Baby for permission to ask Pauline to marry him. He says, "With no disrespect to the Greenes, nothing would make me happier than to make her a Nyman."

Baby responds in few words. Sure, he offers, but suggests that the two of them are quite young. Why not wait? There is no follow-up by Daniel.

I consider that this is why Daniel had given me such a look when I brought up Baby, but feel embarrassed for thinking so. Surely it was due to everything else.

I feel disgusted with myself for being spared. And why? Is it our genetic closeness that prevented him from destroying me? Was I simply an extension of him? Is it a hatred of himself that rendered me sexless, a stale, skewed mirror image of what he had already come to loathe. He wanted something else, something different. What, then, could I offer as the only known blood relative? I could only take his place, spinning my wheels against the wall he'd hit years before I was even born. There was no way I could have intervened, placed my body between his and Pauline's. But, would I have?

Pauline. Oh, Pauline. Did she know? And, all along? Am I the only one kept in the dark, twisting myself into sterility? Had I really hoped to be her? How utterly obtuse. No wonder she couldn't confide in me. I was thick-headed and immature. Her child self had been cracked open like an egg. The lifelessness with which she roamed the house, the reticence with which she shared any detail, I'd taken it as coolness. The malaise of a teenager outgrowing her family home. The time I caught her halfway out the hallway window on my way to the bathroom in the night, thought it to be so cool the way I gave her a look like I wouldn't tell. I'd thought she was coming back in. Now, I imagine, she must have been escaping. All this time I've thought I was her keeper when I am just an extension of the monster. A limb, a weapon, held in his hand while his other destroyed her. How wrong I have been, my whole life.

I feel chained to the office, to the source of the information. Besides, how could I go out there and face Baby again, knowing what I know now? Surely I will wear it on my face. And so what? I wonder if I am liable to lose my composure, and the thought of attacking him brings a strange heat to my chest.

I creep toward the door and close myself in. As I do so I see that he is out of sight, perhaps somewhere upstairs. I am pacing erratically, waiting for Daniel to pick up his phone. All I want to know is if he knew, and for how long, and for how long Pauline knew, and why I didn't, how I couldn't.

"Yes?" It is his girlfriend, Virginie.

"It's Hillary," I say.

"Yes," she says again, and her voice has dropped significantly.

"Is Daniel home?" I feel as if I am calling a landline, though it is Daniel's personal number. Perhaps this is something they do, share cellphones. Or, she saw my name on his phone screen.

"Hillary," she says. "Daniel has been through a lot, as you know."

I wait for her to finish and she doesn't. She is waiting for me to leave while I am able, before she has to tell me herself to hang up the phone.

"I would appreciate if you let him be," she says.

Fine. I hang up without a word, text Catherine, "Hi," realize what I am doing. Surely I cannot tell her. But, does she already know? I follow up by accepting her offer to work with the dogs. Fixing the car seems a hilarious concern. It is the least damaged of all things.

In a mahogany cabinet behind his desk Baby has expensive gifted liquors. Cognac, bourbon, white rum. So, I will camp out, drink until something happens. Either I will achieve mental clarity, or I will find the relief of sleep. I open a bottle of cognac and take a sip that feels equal to a shot.

Then I return to the documents with the open bottle beside me.

It was only out of luck that he didn't read the adoption papers himself when he was sorting them. Or, perhaps it is time I admit, that's how he is now. If that is so, I am in sole control of his story. I will communicate his final chapter to the world.

The pages make less and less sense as I go, and it is when I notice that so much of the bottle is gone that I feel the way the room has been rocking me, back then forth. The text on the pages is blurred, doubled, and before I'd thought it was an issue of comprehension. There is an angry force inside of my stomach, and my mouth begins to swell with water. I cannot coordinate a turn in either direction, and vomit onto the desktop, on the computer keyboard, the file folders, Pauline's birth certificate. Such a horrid noise comes from my throat. I gag, then vomit again.

It is my own sounds I realize I am hearing, a whining sort of cry, and I am being supported at the back by one of Baby's arms, and he is rocking me just as the room before was rocking, and he is saying, "It's alright," and moving my wet hair out of my face and saying, "It's alright."

12

I'VE BOUGHT TRANSLUCENT cylindrical bottles of a fine white powder to sprinkle along the baseboards in my bedroom and over as much of the garage as possible. The salesperson at the hardware store explained that when the bugs make contact, their bodies will dry out and fall apart immediately. The violence of the product appeals to me. Admittedly it is difficult not to indulge a fantasy: sprinkling this or some more powerful product over Baby in his sleep, drying him out.

I awoke this morning with two more bites: one on my abdomen and another on my thigh. Quickly I wrapped myself in my robe, hurried to Baby's office where I could clean up before he woke. Being in the room had such a changed feeling after the full stop of the night; like yesterday's sour spritz of perfume.

When he pads into the kitchen, I again feel the same strange heat in my chest that I felt in his office. I wonder if I really could hit him, and instead I say, "There's a nurse coming," and turn quickly away so I do not have to see him react. My voice came out just like my mother's: like a knife in the heart.

Once on one of our drives, Baby took me the long way into town to get coffee. I can't remember if I was old enough to be drinking it too, or if I'd have had something like hot chocolate or a soda. I must have been about twelve. Because we circled around the long way, it meant we crossed the train tracks behind the café, and then would cross them again coming back around. As we neared them a second time, the alert light started to flash, which meant any moment the crossing barrier would lower. Baby slowed the car, and we approached at a crawl. "I don't know," he said. We could see the train coming from the left. If we continued at our pace, we would be halfway through when the barrier came down on us. The train would be too close to slow down. "I don't know," Baby said. I watched the way his face didn't move, the way he didn't look to the left to see the train and its diminishing distance. At that time, even more than now, I was fearful of my own voice. It seemed an embarrassment to react with emotion. But something long dormant erupted inside of me and I shouted, "Dad!" and we rolled onto the tracks and past them. Surely we were not in any real danger, because of the guard rail and everything. But the two of us knew, between us, that something had happened there, and we had confronted the idea of what it would have meant if we hadn't made it all the way. It seemed an okay way to go, with my dad. At least then we'd have something special between us. Ah, but now I see the childish yearning so clearly for what it was. Wanting a share of my sister's attention. Wanting at least a reason for my constant unease. It is not without shame I realize I thought she had it easier. She could pinpoint it, say *that's why*.

Doorbell. The home nurse is down on the front steps with a tray of coffees and an oil-stained paper bag of pastries from the bakery in town. It seems an offence that he'd have gone there. I imagine him eyeing the counter girls, ordering in some flirtatious way. I've caught one glimpse of him and already we're enemies? I must relax. I was lucky to get an appointment with such short notice.

When I answer the door he is warmer up close. I came through the house from the garage so he wouldn't see me leaving from there and possibly bring it up to Baby. There are lines around his eyes, his hair is thin and swept into a shape like vanilla cream atop a pie. I try to decide what he will be to me. Nothing, I decide. What else, friends? Not to mention that he will be developing an intimate relationship with the house. The space seems unprepared for new eyes.

In a way I am thankful for the shock of a visitor. I've started to fear the house is making me lazy. I'm gaining weight. It can take me hours to get outside and once I am out I have no desire to go anywhere, especially no desire to work. Even before the wildness of last night, things were stagnating. With someone new in the house I feel tethered, and above all I imagine him getting into my things. Perhaps he will snoop through my desk drawers, find the pages and pages of notes for the memoir, not be able to help himself from commenting. Perhaps he will be my editor. We will work long hours into the night, shaping Baby's story into something lifelike and fleshy, ignoring the real Baby

who withers in another room. Anyway, it's my own nos-
ing around through Baby's documents that is affecting my
view of others. Not everyone is so without boundaries.
And my prize? A large crack through my very foundation.

The nurse is explaining the protocol, that he will
mostly be evaluating today, getting in the routines later.
I've become lost, more or less stopped listening to or par-
ticipating in the conversation. My body in the doorway
prevents the nurse from stepping into Baby's office. He
won't push past me, constrained by the friendliness of
the encounter. It's not that he's going to find anything in
there, anyway. It's just that he might *not* find anything,
and this might serve as evidence of the lack of writing on
Baby's part.

There is nothing in the interior of the house that I can
recall that would be overtly wrong, abnormal, embarrass-
ing. There is an inventory in my head—furniture, textiles,
ceramics. But the bugs. I am almost afraid to look, should I
see all of it in a new light and realize things are worse than
I even suspect. They might be crawling along the edges of
rooms, up onto windowsills, dying in the basins of ceiling
lights. What if, when the nurse enters the room, things are
so out of alignment he reports it to the authorities. Or,
what if, when the nurse enters the room, something inside
of me comes to life and I run for the nurse, wailing, sicker
than Baby, truly being the one needing the nurse, and I settle into permanent care. Well that wouldn't be so bad.

I keep my eyes on the floor to prevent myself from seeing the room in a new way. There is a sort of fluttering in
my stomach, and I'm nervous to manage Baby in front of

a professional. Nervous, too, to speak formally to a professional in front of Baby.

The service that dispatches the home nurses cannot promise that the same nurse will be available for each appointment, and so although they will assign a specific nurse to a client, the person with whom I arranged for the service warned that a nurse may be replaced for one appointment or permanently depending on conflicts in schedule and suggested I be home as often as possible should a new nurse need particular guidance on how to properly assist my father. Meaning, it is recommended that to properly enlist the help of a home care nurse who is meant to relieve me of my time at the house I should spend the same amount of time there as before. Although things will change in that now I will be watching my usual tasks be completed by another person rather than doing them myself. This will put me in a position somewhere between Baby and the professional, which in a way is where I have been all along.

The nurse is straight-backed, and smiles through Baby, shaking his hand. It's as if I expect something like a compliment, for him to reach into his bag and present a book for Baby to sign. Nothing can ever just be as it is. I worry Baby will take a disliking to him. He doesn't like men and doesn't trust them, certainly won't undress before one. He, like me, probably expected a young, beautiful woman.

My skin is itching violently. It is as if Pauline is inside of me and trying to claw her way out. I fear the nurse will get bitten while I am out of the house. I will have to burn the boxes of Pauline's clothes. I will blow-dry the baseboards like the person at the hardware store advised. All of this without either of them noticing. The powder will be the easiest. Baby will believe it is baking soda just like in the fridge. I will invent some persistent smell, maybe fry salmon for dinner.

The nurse is asking Baby if he knows where particular items are located in the house. Baby defers to me, I answer.

"In any case," I say to the room, "I have to go."

The nurse does not want me to leave yet. It takes a lot of explaining to tell him about the situation with the dogs, with Catherine, that I am late. He talks about Baby with a certain reverence that reminds me I am the only one who knows about the secret. That the nurse did not enter the house and absorb all that we both know, Baby and me. The nurse asks me what Baby is capable of doing on his own and I say nothing. This, he receives with some offence. I wonder if I am lying, if I could be out for days without Baby noticing, and no emergencies would happen.

"Some things." I correct myself in response to the nurse's expression.

At the kitchen island, I eat a jam-filled pastry and drink one of the cups of coffee with a feeling of guilt and unenjoyment. I finish quickly so I can get to Catherine's before ten o'clock. It embarrasses me to eat something brought by the nurse. It seems to establish his dominance.

MY FIRST DAY WITH the dogs. In my absence from the house I feel that the truth fades. What I learned in Baby's office seems to stay there, tension leaves my body as I drive away. I do have some guilt about not properly preparing him for the introduction of outside help. Surely it all happened so abruptly for him. But then again, most things must. I did not raise the issue with him until the appointment was already booked. Additionally I have not told my mother. She will only push harder for me to move out.

My mother never factors into things for me, with Pauline. See, I always assumed she didn't know. In her presence Baby was quiet, sterile. If I had enough room for my mother in my thoughts I might hate her. I might even see my parents as one in the same. But I don't.

So, the dogs. There are two today: one being what Catherine calls a "regular," and the other a hulking white hound. Catherine is consumed by them. "Bingo!" she sings, patting her legs to call the white dog to her. He slowly obeys. The other, Chuck, the regular, paces in circles.

My job is to help shovel the snow off of her front walkway and then take the dogs up and down the road. Something I neglect to tell her is I have never walked a dog. Sure, I have walked with one. I have friends who I've joined on walks down Queen West with their big calm dogs. But with the leash in my hand I worry I will break some special etiquette. I'll reveal I don't know how to do this, that it is my first time. A thirtysomething, and it's her first time? Imagine if the dogs attack something. A squirrel, or another dog, or a child even. I am ill-equipped. In the face of disaster I will go limp; the dogs will tear me limb from limb and run obediently home to Catherine. They will speak real human words to her about my inadequacy.

The animals nose around whichever room I'm in.
Because now I am suiting up to shovel the front drive, they
are lively, and Bingo is bouncing off my torso with his front
legs, nipping at the wooden handle of the shovel. Catherine
pays them no mind now that they have been transferred
into my care. Sometimes she absentmindedly holds out a
hand; they come to her. Chuck, the smaller of the two and
beige with oblong patches of scruffy brown, has something
going on with one of its eyes, and the corner of its mouth.
Its orifices leak. The wetness around its eyes suggests distress. It walks small circles around the room, stops before
me every now and again and looks into my eyes, looking
like it is crying. "It's okay," I want to say, but I worry I will
be revealing something to Catherine, again. The tone will
give away that I am afraid and inexperienced. She will no
longer trust me with the dogs. And so I look into the eyes
in a way that one might look if they have done so hundreds
of times. I look as if I have not noticed the eyes, as if I have
seen so much that this is within the normal range of my
experiences with the animals. I do it so much that I almost
feel it. That I might love the thing? It paces, and cries. I pull
the shovel free from the jaw of the other.

Through the front window, Catherine gestures toward
areas of the front yard. I shovel them clean as best as I can,
sometimes we do a gestural back-and-forth that takes up
quite some time—more than if I were to go in or she were
to come out—and then I shovel a patch and she shakes her
head, no, and directs me a little in one direction. Eventually
I have cleared a straight path and some offshoot paths,
around back, to the basement entrance, and to the wooden

garbage shed where the big plastic blue and green bins have been snowed in all week, missing Tuesday pickup. There are holes in the surface of the snow where newspapers wrapped in blue translucent plastic have been tossed from the road. Three holes since the first snow, and more newspapers from earlier days buried underneath it. In spring they will be brown and wilted; we'll know everything in them by that point.

The dogs are excited by the yard. They strain at their leashes, and the cold air is making my hands sensitive. The pain of their muscular bodies yanking at the leashes makes me angry and I yank back. I hope that Catherine isn't watching me through the window. Once we are out of view, I unleash them, and they walk obediently at my sides.

Snow rushes at us at an angle, nearly sideways. It finds its way into the little soft centre of my face, through the wreath of fur surrounding it. My hair is wet and the ends freeze into little spikes. It's hard to tell how far we've come from Catherine's; everything is hidden by a sheet of white. The only marker between ground and sky is the road, where traffic has worn down the snow into a brown mush.

I feel a sudden nostalgia for childhood. Or, the understanding of the world I held in those times. I took pleasure in small things, and, well, I do to this day, but now when I feel the pleasure I replace it with a resistance. To get caught up in the smallness is a distraction. Inevitably, should I let myself drift, I would find upon returning that I had missed too much to catch up on. I would find that I had grown slack, ugly, incompetent. Even for a moment. I never let it get away from me. The dogs are like this, though. And none the wiser. If I could live like an animal, if only. Oh, but who is that that says . . . John Stuart Mill? Better to be a dissatisfied human than a satisfied pig, something like that. I guess it has all along been a fallback plan of mine that I may one day become docile. Should the writing not work out. And, here I am with the dogs, it not having worked out. The grief of that all hits me for just a moment, dissipates. Who cares. But so to become limp, it's not such an inferior plan. To be cared for like Baby, to take pleasure in small things once again. To be the satisfied pig. The useless swine. Though the care I envy—Baby's—is my own. If I could feel the comfort of another in the solitude of myself, well then maybe there would be something to that.

We walk up the road, toward traffic like Baby taught me so I can see what's oncoming. My legs feel tight in the cold and so I want to move the three of us forward at a pace that is too hasty for the dogs. I hook into their collars again, pick up my pace. They have work to do; they smell something irregular and they investigate, one of them urinates in the snow and the other buries its nose in the yellow patch, occasionally one turns and looks at me, gnaws at its own leash.

When something goes awry (one dog refuses to walk, there is nipping at my hands or boot laces) I return to feeling that the dogs are aware of my incompetence in a human way. That they not only feel the power shift to them but that they have an understanding of the nuance of my awkward authority. I imagine another person might say— and I think this because I recall Catherine saying something along these lines—that the dogs are teaching some sort of lesson in patience or in experiencing a moment. Of this I feel undeserving, feel that they are not teaching but that they are ashamed of me. I did not arrive an adequate learning receptacle and every lesson is one that I should already have learned. We press on, I continue to disappoint the animals.

WHEN WE GET BACK, Catherine has prepared a late lunch of white bread sandwiches with turkey and butter lettuce. They are on a plate on the kitchen counter where the dogs can't reach them, and she's already eaten hers. I am relieved to eat in private, otherwise I would be unsure of what kind of conversation to make. I have a bigger appetite than normal, eat three halves, and leave the remaining half of the second sandwich in case she had not meant for me to eat both. The dogs tire of me when I am finished eating, and pad one after another into the living room to find Catherine. I wonder if I should stop them, if my being here means they are to be kept out of her sight.

The kitchen sink is a big basin like in a laundry room. I fill it with hot soapy water and begin washing our lunch dishes. Catherine approaches from behind, and startles me by resting her hands on my shoulders. I am struck by a feeling of repulsion, not with her, but with my body and how it must feel in her hands. I feel limp, misshapen. I must stiffen with her touch because she moves to my side, begins to help with the dishes.

I remember—it must not have fully left me yet—when Pauline took me up the steps of the Big Apple on the side of the highway. When we had to sleep so close on a twin-sized mattress in her friend's dorm room that I finally for a short period of time felt I could keep her safe. Then, in the morning, she moved away from me, and I became again unhelpful. When we got home, things were as before.

I think of Pauline and I want to go home, to be alone for a very long time. From Catherine's kitchen window, I can see the trees shake in the wind and create their own little snowfall on the lawn like inside of a snow globe.

"Cabbages are in season," says Catherine. "Do you like cabbage rolls? I might go pick some up and make rolls for supper."

It hadn't occurred to me that I might stay past dinner. Surely Baby will need me home? Time passes easier in Catherine's house. Without the guilt of being out so long, I could stay for weeks.

"I love them. With bacon?" she says. "Fantastic."

I nod. "That sounds great."

A long silence, so I say, "Sorry. Something has been on my mind."

13

WHEN I WAKE UP I am on the couch in Catherine's living room. It is morning, which means I must have fallen asleep sometime after dinner and slept through the night. I am embarrassed to be unaccustomed to the labour of the long walks, the biting cold. After the dogs' second walk last night I lay on the sofa in front of the fireplace, planned only to close my eyes for a minute. Catherine has a way of never interfering. No matter if I told her to wake me, she wouldn't.

When I told her about the awards ceremony, I'd expected a certain amount of validating objection. *Him?* I'd wanted her to say. Instead she had clapped her hands together. "How wonderful!"

I am under a quilt of hers with a cedar smell. The dogs have been put in the basement where they spend winter nights; otherwise things get too muddy with the coming in from the cold. The rugs Catherine lays down when the temperature drops make everything indoors a little softer.

I feel at times that she achieves intimacy with me through her house, as an extension of her self. She makes an effort to provide comfort, insists that I use things, borrow them, and so on. But more often than not we are in different rooms, or held in one place by necessity—a meal, a task such as stuffing a duvet. And we do talk. When she wants to talk we talk, and in those moments there is a closeness. When it's there it's as if it was never gone and when it's gone, well, the opposite is true. In this way I wonder if there is something unfair in our dynamic, and then I chastise myself. She gives me so much. And besides, enough is enough. I know the ins and outs of my complications with Baby. I can't have another person whose behaviours I have to be wary of.

The closest thing to perfection is a relationship unexamined. With distance there's room for so much. Then, a person speaks, and it is all wrong. With each moment experienced of a person they are breaking apart their own caricature.

Think of an iconic figure like Jesus. The same handful of images of him—illustrations, figurines, his face carved into stone on the facades of buildings—shown to us over, over, over. There is a collection of features that make up each representation, unifying each one despite their differences: the long brown hair, the moustache and beard. Sometimes he is draped in fabrics, other times he is undressed and nailed to a crucifix. Sometimes he is handsome, sharp-featured, even modern looking, other times he is soft, young, blushing. He wears leather sandals, a red robe, a crown of thorns, holds a baby lamb. I saw these things in my early years the way I saw trees, sky, road signs. My family was nonreligious; this man meant nothing to me.

I became a compulsive buyer of Jesus paraphernalia in my early twenties. Probably because Pauline at the time was dating a drug dealer with a big portrait of Jesus across his back.

"Are you a Flannery O'Connor fan," Baby joked at dinner. We didn't get it. Years later when I came across the story "Parker's Back," I understood, became once again fixated on the image of Jesus, in particular when it was tattooed on skin.

I have to admit I never spent much time alone with him. Jesus, I mean. I didn't read about him, knew nothing of his teachings, heard somewhere he was *actually a real man*, and didn't investigate. To me he was like anything that decorated walls and candle holders and keychains in gift shops. He may as well have been a flower or a character in the alphabet.

But so I found a set of coasters in a second-hand store in Parkdale, in Toronto. Each one was printed with a different picture of Jesus, and there were six. On one of them, a close-up of his head and shoulders, no cross or crown in sight, I noticed something seemed off about him. He looked like a different kind of person entirely, unlike any depiction I'd ever seen before. For, there was a way I thought him to look. Under all of the robes and hair, without the background of angelic sky. But on the coaster, it was like he was missing whatever it was about him that made him himself. I then examined the other five images. The closer I looked the more his signature . . . something . . . began to fall away.

I could no longer remember what it was about Jesus that made him recognizable to me. What made him Jesus and not someone else with that sort of hair, that white cloth, those brown sandals. On Baby's old desktop computer I searched through databases of images of Jesus—descending from the sky, cross-legged on pale grass, surrounded by angels. This new, off-looking quality appeared in every image. Or, I should say, a different off-looking quality. In different photos he looked unlike himself in different ways. It made me wonder if I had ever even looked at him, before the coasters. If I had seen so many images of him in the years before I became aware of who he was that I had at one time invented something and projected it onto every image I saw of him moving forward, and never truly looked again, becoming more and more wrong in my image of him as more time passed since the last time I actually looked. And this vague, caricatured image I had of him was really a combination of every initial image I saw of him layered over one another and then distorted by memory, by remembering and re-remembering. But there is no original, no way to refresh myself. Each characterization is as wrong as the next, and the person I made by mixing so many together exists only inside of me. I wonder if I do this with everyone, if I do this with Pauline now in her absence; if I have iconized her, made her to look one way, borrowed from one single memory, and she never really was that person for longer than one moment, and never to anyone else but to me. I am afraid that the special secret person Pauline is to me is simply not real, and never was.

So, with Catherine, I don't push it. I saw a powerful image of Catherine in a small frame on her bedside table once: she is smoking, wearing a leopard-print coat and red lipstick, her hair is in a ponytail and she has bangs, grown out a little and parted on either side of her face. Once I saw this, it cemented as the innermost Catherine for me. I see this image in her steps and movements. It is a Catherine preceding even the one I observed in childhood. Before she met Baby, maybe.

I guess I stirred, because there is creaking upstairs. After minutes she appears on the staircase, in an athletic-branded pullover sweater. There is none of that photograph in her. She is middle-aged, private.

"Sorry," I say. "I didn't mean to stay."

She is unbothered. Her day is the same whether I am there or not. I can't imagine. For me, the presence of another swings things out of control.

Together we have coffee and peach Danishes from a Tupperware container. The flavour of the pastry is familiar and I suspect it might be from the superstore in town. Also on the table is a reheated apple crumble, though neither of us spoon any onto our plates. It came out of a white cardboard box with a logoed sticker I recognize from the Big Apple in Colborne, Ontario. A gift forgotten in the freezer? I am struck by the apple crumble and its proximity to my recollection of my trip to Kingston with Pauline. Sometimes I feel Catherine is inside of my head. I have a feeling that she is doing extra to make me feel good, and I feel soft. Decide not to rush out as quickly as my instinct might urge.

Now, I return. She must have sensed that I had left my body, carried on quietly with breakfast. She is eating a second pastry, and has refilled her mug with coffee and cream. If I don't pay attention I follow her with food sometimes, forgetting that she has nearly six inches of height on me, and she really gets moving with the dogs. I worry the distance from the city will make me indulgent. The wine, the heavy cream, my growing habit of watching television. I'll return with the comfortable matronly body of the sexless woman. Or, I won't return. What's worse?

I am startled by my realization of the time. The nurse should have arrived only minutes ago. I imagine a series of crises taking place in the night, in my absence.

"Thanks," I say. "For breakfast, and for everything. The work."

She reaches for the beaker of coffee to refill our cups and I wonder if she's uncomfortable. It's always her, the one being direct. Is it possible she doesn't know how to receive my gratitude? Is it possible she is so comfortable with me because she assumes I won't express it? As if my inadequacies keep her safe. I'm getting too far into it again.

"You were in distress," she says into her coffee. "The car."

The word startles me: *distress*. I'd thought I was so cool that night, that we ran to each other, excited to meet in the night. Now I try to remember it and the scene is darkened. Is it that she'd only been feeling sorry for me?

WHEN I CALL HOME, the nurse answers, won't put Baby on the line. It might confuse him, he says. Suddenly I am a stranger to the goings-on in the house.

"There was a call for you," he says.

"From Baby?" I ask. Perhaps a moment of clarity.

"There was a phone call yesterday before dinner. A niece."

"Oh," I say. "What was the message? Did she say she wants to meet?"

"No," he says. "No message."

"No message? What did she say?"

"She said"—he pauses, seeming to want to be off the phone—"that she is a niece."

"Not of mine."

"No, not of yours."

"Okay," I say. "But no message beyond that."

"No message beyond that," he says.

14

THE COORDINATOR OF THE creative writing program
has suggested a bistro near campus where he has made a
reservation for lunch. Two or three times before leaving
the house I debated whether or not to bring with me the
manuscript in its current form. It is in a three-ring binder
labelled, vaguely, *Memoir*.

A host directs me to a table in the middle of the bistro
where Terry is seated with a mug and a tray of creamers.
There is another mug opposite him, which he fills when he
sees me.

I place the binder on the floor, leaning against the leg
of my chair.

I feel under-dressed, and conscious of my looks. I
should have at least put on a face. When I returned home
from Catherine's, Baby was set up in front of the TV. He
had not much to say about the nurse. The house, though,
was tidy and as if there had been no visitor. I crept through
rooms and sprinkled the bug-repelling powder in cracks
and crevices. I brushed it under my pillows, along the foot

of my bed. After my shower, I took my blow-dryer into my bedroom and blasted the baseboards with heat.

Before I've had much of my coffee, Terry orders us some wine and a tasting platter.

"And how is your writing going?" he says.

"I work here and there," I say. "But there's often something else to do."

A wooden board of meats and cheeses and pickled vegetables is placed between us. Our glasses, filled.

"That is how it is, isn't it."

When we've finished the bottle, poked oily seasoned olives out of a ceramic dish with toothpicks, squeezed lupini beans out of their shells, buttered warm bread, he orders another round of coffee.

"So," I say.

He nods, as if he has been waiting for me to address the binder.

"I wanted to run something by you."

I've placed sticky notes in the manuscript to highlight passages about Baby's various relationships with students, one or two of them underage. I've kept the writing vague, for now, but I have plans for a future revision. Nothing about Baby is vague, or restrained. He is a serpent. I try to picture him back then, his anxieties, feelings of care, and acts of kindness. I can only picture a serpent, winding through the halls of the institutions. Constricting around young girls' throats.

When Baby was accused publicly of courting young students, and this is a story he was always so quick to tell around a dinner table, he claims he looked the head of the

English department right in the eyes and said, "Wouldn't you, if you could swing it?"

But I haven't put that in. In a way, I am testing the waters. I ask the coordinator if he feels one of the students is too identifiable, or if the institution might suffer consequences, even after all of these years.

He reads for a long time. I have to wonder if he is reading multiple times, though it is hard to tell from the movement of his eyes just where he is on the page.

At last, he says, "So it's you who is writing the book?"

I nod. Even here I worry Baby will overhear.

"Well I don't think it should be the climax, the campus affairs. Not if the work is a memoir. And, if they are included, I feel they will be. They will draw quite some attention to themselves."

"Were they not a large part of his career?" Of course I know they weren't a large part to Baby. To him they were . . . what did he call them? Fluff. Am I being greedy, trying to vindicate them too?

He looks to be thinking, or performs it. "Not temporally. Not emotionally, really. I don't think he knew how to care for them. He tried to, and his wires got crossed. He didn't know what to do with the relationship."

"Hm," I say. "Well the real climax would be, I guess, his relationship to my sister."

"Ah."

I wait for him to go on, and he doesn't. His demeanour now has changed. Before, I suspected he was happy to see me.

"I'm just trying to write the truth," I say.

He arranges the bowls and small side plates on the cutting board, tidies everything up. "I'm sure you know best," he says.

He appears to me in a new, perhaps sinister, light. He remains loyal to Baby, no matter what. Yes I can protect Baby with the writing. I can write nothing, or I can write lies, and he will be spared. But what about me? I am an extension of him. Together we are one long winding serpent with two heads.

"I only worry I will regret what I write," I say.

"When a person does something they regret it's because they don't know who they are," he says.

"I have no idea who I am," I say.

THE NURSE IS AT the house giving Baby a bath when I return home. It is an act of pure humiliation. He is undressed, led by hand into the bathroom, lowered into the tub, and so on. The nurse must be so completely heartless to take part in all of this. Just let a person suffer alone, with stoic masculinity. At least in the hours of wasted time during which Baby tries and fails to perform simple tasks on his own, there is a nobility in that. I am the one who brought in the nurse. I have neutered my father. If only someone had done it much, much earlier.

To purge myself from the house, I go to Catherine's. See if there's something I can do even without the dogs, and call it work.

THERE HAS BEEN ANOTHER fresh snowfall overnight.
Two nights ago I awoke when the sky was at its darkest,
watched the flakes dance around the glow of the yard light.
I felt the anxiety of the weight of the approaching morning.

The dogs now have learned our routine. It's the two of
them for now, and I have some anxiety about whether there
are newcomers on the way. Catherine rises out of bed, uses
the bathroom, pulls pyjama pants up over the bottom of
her nightgown, and passes off the dogs to me. She has slept
in—it is nearly two o'clock. It is peculiar how she seems to
mimic my inner state.

I take the dogs outside. It's hard for me to believe
they're not cold out there. I suggested coats but Catherine
says it's demeaning. Anyway, I don't know about dogs.

The snow is deep and I haven't shovelled since last snowfall. The dogs trudge through, and I take big cartoonish
steps, lifting my boot up and out of the snow, then crunch-
ing through the surface in front of me with another step.
Snow gets packed into the top of my boots, around my
calves, where it burns my skin. There's a silence to the out-
doors despite there being wind, the sound of our steps,
the occasional whine of one of the animals. I have grown
accustomed to them. Free of leashes—I have them hooked
onto my belt where they hang dumbly by my calf—they run
free in the snow.

Now, just as I think of silence, something comes
through. A low rumbling, and the dogs perk up. There is a
bit of a flurry, which stings my eyes and bites at my cheeks.
The sound increases, then a figure in the white darkness
of the evening. A truck lurches forward into my field of

vision, honks with the low steady hum that I realize is
being quieted by my state of shock. Its true volume blasts
through and I am shaken back into the moment, my eyes
focus. The big white dog has been hit. Moving wildly, he is
bleeding from the middle and the legs. Upon impact he did
not make a sound. Or, I can't remember. Did he? Now I
assign a sound to the moment. Now I can hear him clearly.
He is convulsing and the other dog is acting dumb and in
the way. I shove the other aside, say, "Don't."

There is nothing for me to do. What, carry him back?
Oh, he suffers.

What I have on me is: the thick leashes I'd never
attached, my cellphone, my keys. I don't know how far
from Catherine's we are but we are far, and my disorien-
tation means I might initially go the wrong way, get even
farther before I realize. A sound comes from the dog's
mouth like fireplace bellows. I imagine, in retelling, someone might suggest, *What did you say?* And so I speak, "Is
anybody out here?" Of course I am alone. We are alone.
The dog with the leaking face, the dog with the bleeding
body, myself. He is in great pain.

Once Pauline compared herself to an injured dog. "The
pain can't stop and no one will stop it because I cannot
communicate it properly," she said. "If I could communicate it properly they would never let me feel this. They
would suspend the laws and let me go."

"Pauline," I say, into the empty air. The truck is long
gone.

I take the thick rope of the one dog's leash—the smaller
of the two—and tie it around the belt of my jacket, and

clip the other end to the dog's collar, and I take the other
dog's leash and I hold it in both hands and I place it around
the tensing, jerking neck of the injured dog and I cross it
over itself and I pull as hard as I can and I choke the dog
until it does not move. This takes all of my strength. But
the dog moves again and it makes a horrible sound. I think
that I am not strong enough to apply the force required to
strangle the dog to death. The small dog is acting limp,
and I wonder if it fears me. I wonder how much of what
I am doing can be comprehended by the small dog. There
is blood on the body of the injured dog. Blood must do
something to an animal, must inform it of something.
Perhaps the dogs cannot tell me apart from a vehicle. Or,
they have forgotten. All that is left is a sign of violence.
In their memories it was me running down the centre of
the road, smashing into the dog. My hands are tingling
from the cold and I go to put them in my pockets but I
remember the dog. I'm surprised by my own ability to forget the dog's pain, and then I remember and I feel it too.
Urgent. Again I wrap the leash around the neck. This time
the dog knows the act, anticipates what I will do next. And
so it strains against me, but it cannot move much and so
it is no match for the smallest of efforts of mine to secure
the rope. With a similar amount of strength to last time,
and I cannot pull harder as now my hands are colder and I
am tired from the previous attempt, something in the dog
relaxes, seems to have submitted. Either it was me or simply the passage of time.

   Now seems too late to call Catherine. Before I worried
my inaction would be seen as a fault. That my waiting

would be the thing that killed the dog. Now I am the thing that killed the dog.

The small dog was not secured properly, and so breaks free, moves a bit to exercise its freedom, then stays by my side. Nowhere to go. So, the two of us stand and stare at the dead dog with the leash crossed over its throat like a rosary made of dirty wet rope.

It is when I realize that the dog is reminding me of my mother that I recall the nights when she shared my bed with me, when the bedroom doorknob would click and release, the sliver of light coming through from the hallway would widen into a yellow rectangle, and Baby would enter the bed, on top of my mother. If she put her arms out straight in front of her, whispered, "No, no," he would put his hands around her neck, and quietly finish his job.

"I have the small capable hands of a bookmaker," he wrote. "Too short for ivory," and I can't recall the next line.

"I stick thick spines in backs." Something like that?

Oh how it comes to me at a faster rate now. It's as though the more he forgets the more I remember. If only I weren't in the house with him perhaps it wouldn't get to me. I wonder if there are enough years left in my life to forget about Baby entirely, were I to leave.

I long to be back in the middle of that specific night, two nights ago, not knowing what I know now. Sure it is a relief, in a way, but what evilness it takes to consider it as such. Questions begin to take shape inside of me, then fall away, exhausted. Finally, my lifelong, "why not me?" is answered.

RETURNING TO CATHERINE'S WITH one dog, I go in the side door with direct access to the basement, where the dogs sleep at night. It is quiet in the house, which I take to mean Catherine is up on the top floor in her study. When she is in there, it's as if she's in another world. She forgets time, transcribes each thought she has in a day in a document. I hope for that, so that I can collect myself before fetching her, but I imagine waiting until she is finished and the delay feels unbearable.

The dog tip-taps its way down the stairs, disappears out of sight. I hang its leash on a hook—one of four along a blue board by the door—and it occurs to me that I might have been able to concoct something. Hang up the two leashes, leave the door open a crack, have it seem that the dog escaped in the night. Oh, same difference. The details of the scene will stay with me until they get fuzzy, until the memory becomes a sentence, until I have become the new person who lives afterwards. Maybe I will become uncaring.

She was not, after all, in the attic study. Pleasantly she emerges from the living room, smiles at me with her lips closed.

I am able to produce words such as *the* and *dog* and I am able to make sounds of stalling and stuttering with no story coming together. When I recall the events I see nothing but snow, and when I recall the strength of tightening the leash I see my boots, and how I had to tug to get them on before I left, how I yanked at the laces to tighten them around my feet, and then snow, snow.

Catherine seems at all times to have an awareness of where the dogs are, when they are in her care. And so by

the sound of the one dog circling in the basement, finding a place to lay and sleep, she was alerted to our return
from a walk that went later into the evening than expected.
The windows are beginning to darken into mirrors.

I have not felt this way in adulthood and so am
unequipped to even employ a tone of voice with which to
deliver the information. "Something," I say, and I am startled by my voice in the silence and the way that it cracks
and goes hoarse and so cough to clear whatever it is out of
my throat and say, "Something happened."

She is downstairs before I can follow up with anything
and then she is back up in the living room and there's a hot
sort of blur as I'm following her from room to room plead-
ing and she hasn't even heard a thing about what happened
yet! But she knows, she can see it in me and besides where
else would the dog be and I hadn't noticed upon returning
to the house that there's blood on me, on my jacket and on
my right hand between my thumb and forefinger, and it's
actually my own from the roughness of the rope, and she
shouts, breaking me out of my panic, "Was he in pain?"

Dumbly, I shake my head.

"Did he suffer?" she says, at the same startling volume.
Her face has drained of colour.

"It happened partway," I say, "and then I made sure it
finished fast."

She turns quickly out of the room. Perhaps in this way
she is protecting me. To react, and later return. The protection, however, will not be worth it if the trade-off is I lose
her forever, which I feel I have already done. The dogs are
not hers but in a way they are, and she tried to make them

mine, to make them ours, and I have killed one of them with its leash.

This instills a sort of mania in the house. Catherine does not want to talk about the dog. She insists that we instead go to bed (it's not even seven, I notice on the wall clock), and there is such an absence of any impulse to act in any way inside of me that I consider this to yes be the only reasonable course of action and I go upstairs and lie on top of the quilt on Catherine's bed with my clothes on and the spot of blood still on my right hand and she goes back to the pullout couch in the living room and immediately my body relaxes so heavily that I know I will fall asleep so quickly and so deep. In this way I am protected for a while from all things.

IT COULD HAVE BEEN hours into the night that I slept straight on my back on top of the covers in my clothes or it could have been one minute that I was out and then there was a banging on the side door that in my half-sleep I knew was a gunshot, and it was Pauline having stacked books of Baby's on top of her chest and somehow with an arm longer than an arm can be she pointed a gun straight against the top of the stack of books and fired. Then my eyes open.

But the bang was the soft click of the bedroom door and the weight on my chest was Catherine's hand. She sits on the edge of the bed, touches me gently.

"You did what was right," she says.

I say nothing. I am feeling so evil that to hear my own voice would be to hate myself even more.

"I'm sorry I didn't say it earlier. I do love those dogs."

The dog in the basement is suddenly disturbed, barks and claws violently at the basement door. He, too, knows that what I did came from a place of weakness.

PULLING INTO THE DRIVEWAY as if back from a long vacation, I dread going inside. Dare I say I wish things could go back to how they were before. A secret simmering, Baby's impending release from his body, my slow wilt toward middle age. I had fantasies not long ago of settling into a forever. That is to say, there would be a notable separation between the first half of my life, through which I have been scattered and upsettable, and the latter half that I long expected to be consistent in tone, pleasant. A single image of a garden, a kitchen, a different, softer sun rising over my head.

There is a nurse—a new one, an older woman—bent over Baby at the kitchen table, fastening the buttons on his shirt for him. I feel no patience for the scene. Baby plays dumb with the nurse, feigns utter uselessness. Or, I neglected to notice the majority of his needs. He is eating a pastry with a soft round slice of peach like a yolk in the centre. Just like at Catherine's.

"How's everything going?" I ask both, or either of them.

"Fine," says Baby. First I wonder if he is embarrassed, but I realize he is angry with me for leaving him overnight. I am angry with him for countless things, nearly everything.

There is a note tucked under the telephone by the front door.

Merle Gagnon

1:30 p.m.

555.319.9539

I must have missed it the other day. Or, she called back?

Her surname means she must be the daughter of Baby's sister, rather than brother, or she herself is married. If she is a niece she is around my age. Married, children, house.

What if Baby has seen? I feel the nurses are conspiring against me, and have to remind myself the message would have meant as little to them as any other.

The round button on the front of the telephone console is flashing green. One new voicemail. I dial with my back to Baby and the nurse, concoct some false message to pretend to have heard in case one of them asks. Imagine the freedom of a household in which nobody asks.

The message is from the other connection I reached out to, the cousin. She doesn't leave any information about herself, but she sounds past middle age. She has not heard of a baby adopted out of the family at that time, isn't familiar with "Baby Davidson"—she said it like that, like it's in scare-quotes—and wonders if perhaps the DNA testing site has made an inaccurate connection.

I am unsurprised, as if this is what I've been expecting.

Neither of the connections has heard anything of an adoption, of even anything of Baby! A great Canadian literary talent. How couldn't they have? Again I am alone with him, his only blood. Their ignorance feels feigned, threatening. It's as if the world is conspiring against him, leaving him to die.

"Hard at work?" says Baby.

I can't help but look at him in disbelief. He is present enough to needle me, though needs help getting dressed. It is as if this will be the last quality he retains. On his grave they will carve *Hard at work, Hillary?*

"Dogs," I say, and it is all I can muster. I feel boxed into the room, and the nurse's eyes are on me. She could never understand the violence of Baby's simply being in the room. To her I must seem hostile, irrational.

"Those dogs get better treatment than most humans." He laughs, looks at the nurse. The nurse doesn't seem to notice, and continues wiping crumbs from the table into a paper towel. "We used to let our dog go out all day, come back at dinner time for kibble."

"I know about Pauline," I say.

"Pauline," he says. He seems to be cheered up by the mention, drops the act.

"She's not yours!" I say, and it is so loud, and so surprising, that I recoil.

For a moment there is nothing on Baby's face, then a certain softness that reminds me of my mother, for the first time. Something he must have adopted from her, from all of the years that he looked at her. Then he explodes into laughter. He takes a bite of the pastry and his laugh is stifled by his closed mouth, but he can't contain it, and crumbs drop from his mouth onto the table. He laughs hysterically in this silent way, unable to catch his breath, pats his hand on the tablecloth.

The nurse clicks the clasp of her bag. "Well," she says. "That will be all for today."

"Thank you," I say to the nurse.

She looks up at me with a skittishness, like I might lash out at her, too.

There is a moment where we all are silent. The nurse gets her things together, moves toward the door. Baby and I wait. He has a wetness in his eyes from the exertion of the laughter. When the door clicks, I lose steam. Suddenly I am in Baby's world again. I am a child, and I am stupid. I don't know what's right. I am meddling in waters beyond my depth.

"You've always been too quick for us," he says.

Never in my life has my father told me I am intelligent. How dare I enjoy it.

"Going out," I say to Baby, to break through the layer of my inner world. Situate myself in the room with him. Allow him not to be who I know him to be. This way, I give both of us a chance to continue on.

He nods, takes himself into his office. He has an air of lightness, and I wonder if he has forgotten. See, I knew he would sooner or later. That is the cowardice of my confrontation. I would have to tell him every day for the rest of his life if I wanted him to know it.

Without the pressure of him in the room, I can think again. I begin to gather my wallet, my keys, a sweater from the coat closet.

I can hear Baby place his house shoes on the mat by the doorway. I know what he is doing. Don't laugh. When he is upset with me he changes into a suit. It began when he started to lose his memory. He will go into his room and come out in a suit, and carry on doing whatever it is he would normally be doing. Once, at the worst of it, he even got into the shower wearing the full suit, washed his hair, and came into the kitchen soaking wet and leaving tracks on the floor and dark wet patches on the kitchen chairs. Then he went to bed in it and in the morning he was back in plainclothes and the suit was dry and folded in his closet, as if leaving it out would be evidence of his behaviour. The whole time, I never said a thing, and in this way the problem became mine. How could I blame him now? It's not as though I asked him to take it off. It's not as though I asked him if it were a direct act of aggression. I simply speak the language of Baby, and I suffer for my fluency. However, I remember my mother. The journal entries about my coldness, her inability to read me. It is possible that I have created these stories. I am the evil showrunner casting a light on everyone around me. Crafting narratives out of innocent whims.

Now there is a rustling from upstairs. I've been keeping my back turned so as not to have to face him. The house is quiet and I have learned the sounds of Baby's routines. He is changing. This, at least, vindicates me. Another repetition of the pattern of punishment for my having upset him. So easily I have backed off, and I wonder if I am wrong.

Baby comes downstairs and he is wearing the same clothes as earlier. This truly enrages me. So if I was wrong about this, have I pinned other things on him? I need someone else in the house. A referee. Not those reticent nurses. I need my mother, though she is too much. She so harshly characterizes him that I end up speaking in his defence.

And so there is no middle ground. I am the enemy of my parents, and the enemy of the world.

I leave without comment.

I DON'T KNOW WHERE to go. There is Catherine's, but I don't want to tell her what I know. Not yet, at least. There is a place down the road from Catherine's where sometimes visitors will leave their vehicles. An empty lot with a path straight down to the water. Usually in summer there will be swimmers down there who come from some of the lots with the bad beaches. In winter, it sits empty.

I drive down to the lot and park next to an empty pickup truck, flash my lights to see if anyone is wandering around outside. What's funny is normally I'd be worried about a break-in or someone dangerous finding me and becoming violent. But in the dark on the empty lot, facing the frozen lake but unable to see more than a few shadows of trees, I want nothing more than to see another person, to confirm that I am not entirely alone on an empty planet.

We used to swim here when the leeches would get bad in the water by our own place. One summer Pauline told my parents she lost her bikini top when she went to the beach with friends, and tried to stay home when the family was going to swim at the empty lot. Really, I saw that she flung it up on the roof; a strap hung down and I could see it in the yard, bright fuchsia in the afternoon sunlight. Our mother was furious. She knew she was lying, or assumed. So, Pauline was made to swim topless. I swam short slow laps back and forth, my father called out the time he kept on a stopwatch, and Pauline stood with her arms crossed, concealing her chest, and stared at my mother on the shore.

Does Baby remember things like this? Were these moments just as any others? I wonder, if I were to remind him of each and every one, if he would then be himself again. If in the moments before he forgot again he would be whole. Whole and bad. And if I don't do that, is he less bad? The incomplete version is a superior one. If he forgets enough, will he perhaps be absolved of his past?

So maybe I should never remind him. He will never fully be himself again, but I will forever be holding pieces of him inside of me, keeping them from him, keeping him good. The more Baby forgets, the more he is free of himself, and the more the stories belong to me. Though surely there is a difference, there does not feel to be one. It is me who becomes bad.

I resign myself to sleep as long as possible, decide what to do with the darkness once I've had some rest. The seat only goes back so far, so I curl to one side with my hands under my head, wrap my coat as tightly around my body as it will go.

I am woken from a dream by the pain of the low temperatures. The car starting up is louder than it's ever been; I fear I'm waking something up with me. First the dream hangs around like a feeling in the car, then I remember the animal. The big white dog, slithering into the Jeep through some mysterious hole in the floor, slick with its own black blood, nipping at my hands and feet and face (the cold was making them sting), clambering up onto me in the reclined car seat, scratching at my skin (I'm out of my coat,

in-dream), licking at my neck with its foamy tongue; it has
a knowingness in its movements, a finesse, as if having the
ability to hold me in its hands, to look into my eyes and
emote, and it enters me, and it works away at my body,
thrusting, bringing itself to orgasm, and it ejaculates inside
of me, collapses on top with its limbs around my body like
a human's, and I'm not thinking in such a way as to criti-
cize the humanness or un-dog-likeness of the animal, I'm
feeling the ejaculate leak out onto the seat of the car, and
when I awaken there's that sensation, still, of a wetness
between my legs in my underwear.

My eyes are stinging from the car light. It must be halfway through the night and now more than ever there is
nowhere to go.

SHE MUST HAVE GONE looking for me. So, Baby must
have called, then. Told her what happened. Some version
of it, at least. Again I feel like a child. All this time I've felt
that Baby was in my care, and how easily things reverse.
Catherine has made a makeshift bed in the back seat of her
car: a yoga mat sort of haphazardly unrolled over the seats,
a pillow from her bed, a quilt. I feel upset at the realization that she is offering me her precious possessions. I am
unclean, there is some blood on me, I have let her down.

"Does it hurt?" she says. I see her lift her chin and know
she is looking at me in the rear-view mirror.

I am inspecting my hands, empty of feeling, and blue at
the tips of my fingers. I feel as though I have not spoken in
a very long time. I can't remember the last thing that I said.

"It's okay," I say. I imagine if Catherine hadn't found me, if no one had, how long it would have taken for me to drop in temperature into a state of bliss. To exit the vehicle, move toward the water, to lie alone and flat along the ground with my arms and legs spread, like a person making a snow angel, cars driving off the road and over me, my ribs all lined up in neat rows inside of me, chairs in houses all lined up around the lake with families all lined up around the tables, giving thanks for the food on their plates, and I would move my arms and legs back then forth to dig deeper and deeper trenches down into the ground.

"It only hurts," I say, "when I do this." Her eyes are on the road, but I demonstrate anyway. Squeeze my hands slowly into fists.

Every movement of the car seems to shake my frame, causing pain to vibrate through my bones. We make a sharp turn, then another, then slow down. Catherine lowers her window, loudly places an order for two cheeseburgers, two medium fries, two Pepsis. Then she cranes her neck, asks me, "Anything else?"

"No," I say, and I want to say thank you, but my eyes well up and I start to cry. I think about how Catherine would have set up the same mat, quilt, and pillow, if I had been the injured dog. About how she would perform CPR, say something into the dog's ear and know that it understood. I am one of Catherine's dogs, and she will not let me die. She will never, though, let me not be a dog.

15

SLOWLY WHITTLING DOWN THE list of long missing stretches of time. Mostly I can fill things in from memory, or by using notes and photographs. There are chapters written quickly in point form, almost seeming to mock the severity of their contents in their brevity. "Divorce," one page reads, highlighted in red. "Accident," reads another. Some of it I am rereading for the first time. Some of it I make up entirely.

We are past the point of my asking Baby for any help in piecing things together. Yesterday, I called the landline and he picked up in such a state, interrupting my every word, yelling that he would not allow me to take him away, that I, and others, have long been conspiring against him. I didn't take it personally; he showed no sign of knowing who had called. Luckily—things line up in order sometimes—he has an appointment this week. I've been unable to make up my mind about whether to tell the doctor about the ceremony. Not to invite him, though the thought is amusing. It's just if things carry on like this Baby may not be well enough to attend. And then what? The whole thing falls apart. Perhaps there's something I'm doing wrong, or something I could be doing in addition to what I'm doing right. Perhaps something can reverse this process, at least stop it in its tracks.

Anyway.

There is a highlighted page of information I need from my mother. She has agreed to be interviewed so long as I don't credit her in any way. I hide away in Catherine's office and worry that my mother will know I am there, or worry that, at least, she will ask.

The breathy smell of an unlit beeswax candle is making me uneasy, so I move to the window. Outside is bright and frigid. There is an unblemished layer of snow over the backyard. What if it just kept falling? Do we have the mechanisms in place to control it? I imagine it falling and falling, burying the city with our dull orange lamps and degrading machines. All things would seem very important. Then, all things would disappear. This thought grabs hold of me, reveals to me the meaninglessness of this project for the first time.

The phone is interrupted on its second ring.

"Yes?"

—

Hi.

Hi.

Shall we start?

Sure.

Do you remember the spring of 1978?

Some.

Do you remember a trip out east? There are photos of you under the Hopewell Rocks.

Yes, of course.

Was he working on something at the time?

He was always working on something. The photo you're talking about, if it's the one I'm thinking of, was taken by a stranger. I stopped a man with a baby strapped to his chest. I hadn't seen that much before, you know, back then it was something I'd have noticed. I thought it made him seem nice. Safe. I stopped him and asked if he would take my picture.

Where was Dad?

See that's what I was saying. He didn't even see the rocks. He sat in the car, scribbling in his notebook. Didn't even see the rocks.

How long was he in Toronto, after the Europe tour?

Weeks. A month, maybe. I thought he'd left me.

Did he?

Not in the way I'd thought. He came back.

The dedication in that book—

Ha. Yes.

A.J.? Who is that?

Some kid. Anette Jar . . . I don't remember her name. Jar-something. She was his protégé for five minutes. A grad student at U of T.

Sorry, I shouldn't have brought it up.

She was beautiful. Whatever. Whatever, really. Over and done.

Can I ask you something?

Isn't that what we're doing?

Not for the book.

Sure.

Was he nice, before? To you? Did he used to be nice to you?

Of course. He was the love of my life. He is. He always will be.

Really?

Really. Of course.

What happened?

It's a certain kind of thing, Hill. You know. It's . . . some people. He's not like everyone else. He finds you, he gives you everything, he can't live without you. He finds someone else. It's just like that, over and over.

When did it change?

For me? On and off. He fell in love with me a few times.

You think he's the love of your life?

Of course. But, someone else. Not that man, now. You have to treat these things like a death, Hill. He died. I'm sad for him. I pity him.

[There is a pause.]

Can you remember what happened with a bar fight in 1999? Around Halloween?

A bar fight?

Dad hurt his hand, punching some guy? It was tense at dinner, with his parents, I remember.

He didn't get into a bar fight. He hit a guy. Middle of the day. He went and found him at work.

Why? Who was it?

One of Pauline's friends.

I don't remember him.

One of her, you know, one of the guys she was seeing.

Older?

Definitely. Almost forty if I remember correctly.

Can I ask you something else, off-record?

Is the tape still going?

Yeah, but it's just me. I'm not going to transcribe it.

It's not off-record if the tape is going, you know.

**It's just the machine is old. Sometimes it gets messed up
if I stop and start.**

Okay.

How come you used to drive her to all those guys' places?

All those old guys?

I was everyone's chauffeur. I drove you girls all over.

I mean, you know what I mean.

[There is a pause. A sound that is either in the background,
or a thinking sort of hum.]

I wanted her to have a chance.

At what?

At normal stuff. Normal sexuality.

[There is a pause.]

What do you mean?

No, I mean . . . I wanted her to develop an understanding of
how men are.

I don't think I understand.

I don't know, Hill. I just did what she wanted.

[There is a pause.]

She wanted a ride, I drove her.
Because you were afraid of her?
No, I wasn't afraid of her. I was . . . no.
Afraid of her having too much to hold against you, I mean?
I just did what she wanted.
Why didn't you tell me about her?
About her?
You know.

[There is a pause.]

Hillary, because then you'd have hated her too.

—

THE INTERVIEW IS A long bar, spiky and black, grow-ing thicker and angrier as it moves toward its sudden end, where it drops off. I transfer the file to the computer, scroll to the end, and split the clip. Delete the last portion.

I can make anything of the conversation if I cut and arrange it. Similarly, I can do this with the memoir. I can do this with my life. Is that not, after all, what my mother has done? She erased, erased. She shaved down the spiky edges, showed me a quiet flat line.

No one ever wanted me to feel anything. No one even wanted to hurt me.

What sort of experiment was I, and what was Pauline?

I make a note on the back of the photograph of my mother under the Hopewell Rocks: *Dad behind camera.*

I highlight the interview in its entirety, and erase it.

Pauline's truth is gone, and Baby's truth is gone, and every truth that existed between them, gone. The dog, too. I have told the half-truth of its accident, how it ran out in front of the truck. My own hands have been omitted from the scene. But that is the power of the author, is it not? Behind the keyboard, I can make truth. I can resurrect moments between Pauline and Baby, I can make them true again. More so, even. I can lock them away in the minds of readers all over the world. And then no one will forget, and if they do, they can read it again.

When Pauline was admitted to the hospital at sixteen (I was thirteen) my mother said, "Just tell me, Pauline, what happened to you?"

I'd always thought she just meant the drugs. That she wanted an admission of being acted upon, that someone else was trying to hurt her. Something slipped into a drink. What happened to you meaning, *How did these get in your mouth, who made you swallow them.*

Suddenly, and too late, I understand.

What happened to her? What else, that I didn't see through the opening in my bedroom doorway?

16

CATHERINE IS ALLOWING ME to use the desk in the attic to work on my writing while the dogs rest in the afternoon. There are three of them today, and they're in need of a walk before dinner, but I assume that I have been relieved of my duties. I feel afraid to bring it up with Catherine and instead timidly avoid interacting with the dogs. Besides, it's freezing outside. The animals are better off curled on the rug in the living room. I haven't said much about the project to Catherine, and she hasn't asked. She seems to like having a writer in the house, no matter who, and no matter what they're doing. I've hired multiple nurses to cover the longer hours at the house.

The desk faces out a window from which I can see the backyard, where I am able to identify lumps in the snow as the concrete birdbath, the iron patio table and chairs, the birdhouse that juts so proudly up from the ground, wearing a puffy hat of snow. There is something else creating an irregularity in the surface of the snow. I imagine it is the big white dog, and have to look away.

Catherine's desk is big and heavy, and the top is chipped and stained and has small markings in the wood. Some almost look like words, but I can't make any of them out. In the drawers are small pencils sharpened down almost too small to use, two aluminum pots of the same cherry-vanilla lip balm, old soft notebooks, and a thesaurus and dictionary. Her computer is an old beige desktop with a square monitor. It makes sounds like simmering water when it loads, and there is a few-second delay each time I type a character. All of a sudden the words will come streaming out after I type them, as if I am tiptoeing through the story and then falling into a hole.

I can't help it. When the computer is slow to load, I continue to look through Catherine's drawers. Each item seems sacred. I can't imagine her actually using them, like they are so much part of the backdrop of her world that to single one out would require the interest of an outsider. To her it would be like examining a notch in the wall panelling.

At the back of one of the drawers is a photograph of Catherine and Baby, in our house. They are in front of an award of Baby's, newly mounted on the wall, linked at the arms. Who would've taken such a photo? My mother? Surely not. Behind them on the right I can see the entrance to what I remember as my mother's office, only it is clear from the decor and the furniture that the room is my father's. It is sparse, mahogany, the floor is carpeted. It's not the office in my memory, where my mother kept her books, her bicycle with drop handlebars wrapped in mauve tape. All of her feminine objects, the subtle scent of her

being in and out of a room often. Back then she was so soft,
so barely there unless spoken to, unless alone with just us
girls. It isn't without guilt that I am nostalgic for that time.
Her new power should be something I celebrate. It must be
in the present, knowing my mother as I know her now, that
I project backwards and assign some sort of territory to
her. Really, she drifted from room to room.

From where else could the memory have come—a
dream? All of it, a dream. Memories like a deck of cards,
I can sort through and see my hands before my face in the
room. Feel the patterned blue rug on the floor, the hard
flecks of whatever that got tracked in on our socks. All a
dream. But then, why would a person have such dreams?
Such piercing fear in the air, such sickness at the thought of
opening the office door, and going back out into . . .

The office was a dream, the varnish on the chest of quilts
may have been a dream, the dancing in the living room to
Little Richard could have been a dream, the feelings I feel
to this day, each day, are dreams. But that's all there is. I
ask myself, over and over: if Baby forgets enough will he be
absolved of his past? Memory is all there is. These dreams
are different than others. I can't wipe them away like the
times I've been chased by evil slithering creatures, the times
I've shown up somewhere without my clothes, the times a
series of shapes and sounds have given me a feeling so strong
I carry it with me all day in waking life. In the absence of
those dreams I am awake; in the absence of the others I am
nothing. I would be a pedestrian in the world, for once, I
think. I would be like any other. I could go into the other
room and just sit, not even face the window. I could go

somewhere else, stay a long time. Then, I don't know. By then I would be someone else entirely.

The biggest dream of all is the one in which I had reason to envy Pauline, reasons to fantasize about us swapping places. I am the only one who has ever belonged to him, been kept safe under his protection. I wore a halo of protection, sat back and watched him harm the others.

I remember things one way and then I return and things are different. Scenery evaporating into the air like it's been released by my opening it up to examine. So long as I don't interfere everything remains pristine. Otherwise, I can twist and sicken. For example, all of a sudden one day I took offence to Baby having worn a yellow suit to visit Pauline when she was at her most unwell. It was as if he'd been trying to antagonize her. I revisit and it looks clownish, he's laughing. His truck is bigger and it makes a racket when he pulls into the driveway. Though I specifically remember taking a liking to it when he'd arrived. I'd felt it was in line with him being different. He could never just be quiet and do things normally, and the familiarity of this behaviour—the inability to fade into the background—comforted me. And so this change in feeling upon recollection was a shade away from a change in memory: assigning a sinister intention. Could I remember anything? Any one thing about him, truthfully. Had he acted at all throughout my upbringing? Surely he could have just as easily stayed perfectly still, in one room in the house, for the extent of my childhood. Surely he could have been—could be, still—a statue. I could have imagined everything else. But not with Pauline. Every moment between Baby and Pauline lives somewhere inside of me, replays in my mind.

I AM NEARLY FINISHED the manuscript. It's not so bad. At least parts of it. It is when I am not with Baby that I'm able to see him with some objectivity. The words come faster, but I worry they are more critical.

I return to the new empty page. It feels as though it belongs to Baby, as if it is already bound in his memoir, under his big bold name on the front cover. I am to write a scene somewhere in his late forties, when he is established but rising. I feel his scrutiny each time I move to begin the passage. Funnily, I look behind me. All alone, I dare to stray. At the top, I type, "by Hillary Greene." Above it, a space for a title. But what? To enter one feels a crime. Sure, I have written before. But only ever played at it. And what if I were to write something great? Something of mine. I type a letter *A*. Well, a start. It is nothing, the idea. At least not yet. But something has happened. A small spark. Now I am pleased, and I put off the work on the memoir, and I go downstairs.

WE HAVE LUNCH TOGETHER and Catherine asks me to read her some of what I've written. She seems not to notice the writing itself, asks questions only about the content. She'll say, "That's a nice moment, with your mother," or, "That sounds just like him," or, "Would Pauline want that in there?"

I feel frustrated with her, as if I'd been expecting praise or recognition of some linguistic mastery. I am beginning to deflate insofar as Pauline's story is concerned. It's possible these ways I've imagined I am doing her a great favour I am really just digging around in her past. Pauline was not a writer; she may not have felt the same redemption through text. Catherine is right: Would Pauline want any of it in there?

When we were young, our mother was always getting involved in our personal affairs. She would storm into our school and negotiate our report cards, intimidate the awards committee. She once told a boy on the playground who had all of Pauline's hair clenched in his hand that she would kill him if he did not let go. Pauline's face went a deep shade of red, and she whispered something to the boy. As if to punish my mother, they became good friends.

I consider taking it all out, telling Baby's story and his story alone. No word about what he's done to anyone else.

When we finish with the dishes and they're set to dry slotted neatly between the wires of the rack, Catherine asks if I'd like to come for the dogs' midday walk.

"Although I guess you've got more work to do," she says.

"No," I say. "I could take a break."

We divide the dogs between us, one with me and two with her.

"Actually," I say, looking forward into the wind, "I thought of something today."

She sniffles, uses the back of her mitten to push at the tip of her nose. I take this as a cue to continue.

"A book, I think."

"What is it called?"

"I don't know yet. A something. I know it starts with *A*."

"A something," she says. "Now *that's* it," and we laugh.

I KNOW THAT WHEN we get to the place where the dog was hit, the body will not be there. I think that I do not believe any of the events that happened that day. And so of course there is no body. Of course there is not a mark on my jacket. I invent many things. Surely I embellish stories. The moments with Pauline, for example. Did Catherine not like that I wrote them in because I exaggerated them? She was around for some of it, too. She knew what was going on. She, too, did nothing.

Together we walk the same route I took with the dogs.

We pass irregularities on the other side of the road in the snow and I think I see parts of an animal emerging from the surface, but I do not. Then, I do. There is blood in the snow in a pattern of splotches. The body, however, is not there. The presence of the blood makes the dog feel more alive to me than before. Not as alive as when it was living, but more alive than in my memory of its death. It confronts me with the closeness of the event. As time goes on, the closeness of the event and of this present moment will become greater, until they have merged into one memory, the day of and the day after. Each moment is as far as these events will ever be, more time layering over top and compressing time into a flat straight line.

I wait for Catherine to go up ahead, from where I can hear her chattering happily to the dogs. With the leash looped around my wrist I take handfuls of the bloody snow and put them in the pockets of the camping jacket I borrowed from Catherine. I pack it in until they are full, and wet spots grow at the bottom of the overstuffed pockets. Once the snow melts out, the blood will stay.

The pockets are too full to be fastened shut with their snaps so I tuck the edges of the flaps around the snow and put my cold wet hands inside of my sleeves and quicken my pace to catch up with Catherine and the other two dogs.

WHEN WE GET BACK the snow has melted through my pockets, left wet streaks down the front of my coat. Catherine runs her fingers through her hair, pulling clumps of snow and ice. She hangs up her coat and it drips small puddles onto the floor in the entranceway, eases into the warmth of the living room.

The door leading to the basement is ajar, and through the gap I can hear the sound of multiple chewing mouths. I tap my nails on the wood and downstairs the dogs stir.

They accept me into their territory, contrary to my anticipation that they might now act aggressively in my presence, without Catherine. All three stop eating when I reach the bottom of the staircase. In a state of fear I surprise myself by saying, "I am sorry," to Chuck. He rises on his legs, comes to smell something familiar about my coat.

"Sorry," I say, and I pat his head. He digs his snout into the fabric of the camping jacket, against the bulging wet pockets. The majority of what is in them has not yet melted, but enough has that the material of the pocket is soaked and dripping. There is a faint hormonal smell. The dog fishes around with his nose until he discovers the opening of one of the pockets, and then he eats the contents. I open the other for him, and he eats out of it too. Then I lay down flat on my back and he comes and rests his body against my torso and sniffs at my face and I move his head away and he comes back and sniffs again, and we do this over and over. The other two dogs come over and lie on my other side, and all of us fall asleep.

THE SMELL OF THE basement, the smell of the dogs, and their food. Catherine has her hand on the side of my face and is holding my phone.

"I didn't mean to look," she's saying, "but I saw that it's your mother calling, and I thought you might want me to tell you."

The pot lights in the ceiling are a painful yellow, and one of my eyes feels sealed shut. I've lost track of the time, and down with the artificial lighting it's impossible to tell how long I was asleep.

Catherine is quick to leave the basement, to give me privacy. In part I wish she would stay, referee somehow. If my mother knew where I was she would drive down and take me out herself.

"We've worked out a good day-to-day," I say, about Baby. "Sometimes he's there, sometimes he's not."

"Must be better when he's not," she says, and laughs.

"In a way."

When I tell my mother the anecdote about the bugs, I expect that we will laugh together. Her voice on the line is a relief, a brief opening of lightness. So, I explain the events. The white powder, the blow dryer. What worse surprise than to find something living among the possessions of a dead sister? Well, okay, it's not so funny. Maybe it's pity I wanted. But it was only meant to be a segue. See, I knew eventually I'd have to bring up what I know.

"It might just not be the right time," says my mother. "You know, while they're there." The bugs, she means. She worries I will bring them with me, that they will infiltrate her house and reproduce. How foolish I feel for having assumed I was the one doing her a favour by visiting for the holidays.

"They're not," I say. "Really, I haven't woken up with another bite."

The feeling of the phone call is off now, seems not to invite any sort of closeness. Instead, I invite her to the award ceremony. How stupid. What interest would she have? She'll let me know, she says.

Really I'd been wanting to confront my mother's husband. It wouldn't have done any good, anyway. It's as if I expect they'll congratulate me for putting all of the pieces together. As if I had been clever, rather than Baby destructive.

Baby once told me that the more his work is edited, the less it feels like his—sometimes even someone else's book entirely. "I'm closer to having written the last book I read," he said. So, maybe Pauline didn't belong to the first husband anymore. Maybe it was too painful for him to see her raised by Baby, and somewhere in his mind (or in his heart) he had had to sever something very early on.

Anyway, does the first husband even know? He'd have had to consent to the adoption, no? Perhaps there was more going on. Though I must admit since discovering the truth I've started to see so much of Pauline in him, when I look at the photos in my mother's old albums. I almost feel as though I love him. I remember the last time I saw him and I think, *Ah, just like Pauline.*

I HANG UP. I imagine the nurse speaking ill of me, finding small pieces of evidence around the house that I have been a poor caregiver, an even worse daughter. I still have not called home to Baby. And he hasn't called me. I worry I may even miss him. Not him, perhaps, but the house, and our routines. My relationship to Baby feels inaccessible, as if I am very far away, in time and location. Like he is a character in a book written long before I was born. Baby's life before me feels like one very long day, with one overarching mood. It seems there was purpose to every action, no stakes, that he would inevitably end up here, having daughters, a house, having and losing a wife.

We have tried to contact the dog's owner, who left a relative's number in case of emergency. She is in Rome, the relative tells us, but does not know how to get in contact with her, and does not know when she will return. Without the direct consequence of my action I feel I cannot escape it. I worry I will live the rest of my life in waiting for the woman to punish me with her immense grief. But, she goes for months at a time. She drops off the animal and rarely checks in. It is Catherine who I have wronged.

The least that I can do is find out exactly to what degree I have misbehaved. I look up the internet forums on animal control, on caring for pets, on untraceable killing of living things. A veterinarian in Minnesota says that the kindest way to deal with an injured dog is to shoot it between the eyes with a large-caliber gun, 9mm, point blank. The next best way, she says, is to feed the dog pills, like benzos. When it's out, she says to slit the throat to the bone and let the dog bleed out. Another user suggests the most humane thing is to sell one's personal items in order to pay for humane euthanasia. So, I erred. That's that.

CATHERINE HAS ARRANGED A display in the living room. She is wearing a nice but casual dress: black, cotton, with braided straps over her shoulders. I am surprised by her upper body, her bare legs, which have been so buried under her winter wear. There is soft classical music playing on the radio and it is making me emotional, reminding me of Pauline's funeral service. None of it was personal to her, that's what got to me the most, I think. Now it's a generic ceremony that will forever hit me where it hurts. The living room is reflected in the blacked-out windows. Beyond the blurry reflected furniture, wallpaper, our bodies, is complete darkness. Somewhere out there is the road home.

"Would you like to share any words," says Catherine. On the small side table is a photograph of the dog, its curled-up leash, and a toy; presumably its favourite.

"Um," I say. My face feels hot. I am at a loss for what to do. In the photo, the dog has its mouth open, as if grinning.

"You were a noble character," she says, looking at the photograph. "You held your head up high, and you knew right from wrong."

"I agree and I, well . . . " I look at Catherine, then at the floor. "I think the thing that, well, harmed you, is the same thing that made you so brave. You never hesitated."

What I said was wrong, it was not true, and it wasn't beautiful like what Catherine had said. I never learned how to be like that, is the thing. To just say something and mean it. I worry that on one level Catherine hates me, thinks I am evil. *Knows* I am evil. I feel completely transparent in the room, completely alone, and then Catherine puts one arm around my shoulders, and kisses me.

MORNING. I DON'T HAVE a thing to say on the drive over. How could I? Not an hour ago the sun yellowed the bedroom walls, the linens, it eased us out of one state and into another, more conscious of each other's bodies. I realized I'd been sleeping with her hand flat over my belly, which seemed to pool with its own weight toward the bed; self-consciously I rolled over onto my back, and her hand found its way downward. I'd retired from trying to feel that certain feeling, and all of a sudden there it was. My body cinching at the pelvis, then falling away from itself. In that certain way I feel I must love her. But there are many ways to feel, many ways to be.

We pull to one side of the road that separates the cemetery. Pauline's plot is two rows back, sits proudly in front of an oak tree. Often a flower from another site will blow over to hers, and no harm in letting it stay. The shame is that I don't bring them myself. It's just I feel she'd laugh at me.

"Do you think she'd want me to wait in the car?"

"What?" I say. "No." I want to reach out and touch her, but I don't.

"It's just I was always around, getting in the way."

"She'd want you," I say, but I am unsure of the truth of it.

"I had this sense that every minute I spent with your dad I was keeping him from you two. I imagined I was some sort of witch."

"Oh," I say. "I always felt he was more yours than ours."

She thinks, nods. "He was sometimes. Or, he wasn't really anybody's, is what I mean. It was whoever was in his line of sight at the time."

Now he is mine, I think. Like a taxidermy animal.

"She'd want you," I say.

CATHERINE GETS OUT FIRST, but doesn't know where to go. She is holding herself with a certain reverence toward the place. I imagine if I were to crack a joke, she would be put off. This is the thing about others: they always seem to know what to do. In my hands I have the manuscript, well, part of it. I've printed the manuscript, stapled it, then sealed it in a manila envelope. It was Catherine who suggested the envelope, as if I am sending a letter. I didn't tell her what is in the envelope, that it is an apology to Baby for telling his true story, and to Pauline for not doing it sooner.

You see, acting from a place of revenge had been changing my posture. I had begun to crawl like a rat, I imagine my face must have sat in a sneer when I let it relax. The symptoms of this evil thinking had been pangs: Pauline, Catherine, my mother. I'd tried to convince myself the truth was the truth, told or not. That their secrets belonged to them. That there was wisdom in being dormant, in remaining small, in sacrificing my person. I have long wanted to strip myself of my smallness, but worried to act big in a small world would be a crime. I hold precious objects in my hands, must keep constant watch over them. I had always imagined that chaos was beneath a great precipice, that I would have a thought, for example, *Now I will become chaotic*. I understand the silence of destructive things. And so I must meddle, must enter back into the world from which I came.

Keeping Pauline's secrets has been a long slow act of violence against her. I went so far as to invade her, and did double the harm by letting things be. I would sneak into her bedroom and read her secret writings, and feel pity for myself for my absence in her stories. They were great adventurous stories of her and Baby, a friendship unlike any other. In this vague, juvenile world, they were ageless, without any declared relation, alone in a world that they would conquer again and again. As if, if it were just them, alone with the unspeakable behaviours, things would be alright. As if it had been the real world and its intrusive morality that presented the problem. Without a name for it, the relationship could just be. For this reason I felt my interference would only pull us further apart. How could I be her saviour when I wasn't even a character in her story?

I LEAD CATHERINE TO Pauline and she reads the engraved text, and looks at me. I place the envelope on top of the grave, where deep down there it is unclear to me what remains, if I would recognize any of it. I can't seem to make myself believe it isn't just Pauline in her entirety down there, alive and laughing.

We were never so serious. Even death seemed a joke between us.

Now?

Some things are larger. I am standing at my sister's headstone. Beneath it, my sister. This thought repeats, and distracts me from any sort of romance. How does a person ever stand before a grave site and recite something so foolish as a poem?

Catherine's voice through my thoughts surprises me. Says, "People act in funny ways when they're angry."

I infer that she means my mother's husband, that he left his child, or that she means Baby, in how he treated Pauline, or with Pauline in how she couldn't keep going, or all of it. I don't answer, so that all of these may be true, and are not to be disproven by what she says in response. I remember she doesn't know those things.

We stand close, but do not touch. That is over, we've returned to our ways. It's as if she's gotten something out of her system. I long for us to touch again.

"Okay," I say.

Catherine nods toward the grave.

"Pauline," I say. "I'm sorry I didn't save you."

Catherine waits for me to say more, but I cannot think. To get to more words I would have to sift through more disturbing images.

"She'll forgive you," says Catherine.

I nod. I place the pages, all of the pages with Pauline's stories, on top of where she lies. The book, which started as Baby's, belongs to Pauline. His past, his shallow glamorous friendships, his expensive whiskeys, his books, his awards. All of it takes a back seat. One copy for Pauline and one for Baby, before I give it to the whole world.

"An ugly sort of forgiveness," she says.

Is that true? Until now I've needed Catherine here with me, but when I consider Pauline I can only imagine she would be angry. She did not see Catherine as family. I imagine she did not see herself, even, as family. Seeing how the bare pages of the manuscript disrupt the beauty of her resting place, I regret every word. Was all of this for her, or was it all really for me? Catherine, too, is surely here for herself, no? I have twisted myself into resenting all three of us. I shake my head to clear it of any thought and look to Catherine, who is gazing off into the empty grey distance over the roofs of the main street.

17

WHAT HAS COME OF the memoir, I have to say, is good work.

I made a version—a safe one—without Pauline, just to see how it looks. And, sure, there is much truth in it. A lie is a spoken thing, I tell myself. A lie is active. An omission is something else. Slowly, without a sound, the words work through the book like a snake, slithering from cover to cover, and before a reader knows it they have finished, and without a mention of Pauline. This sleight of hand is at the mercy of the coordinator at the university, of Baby, of Catherine. There is not a word of Baby coming into contact with anyone, anything. As if he is untouched, and more importantly, so is the world around him. He exists as a pair of eyes, as a pair of hands at the typewriter. This is the role of the writer. Funny, that he has not written a word of it.

But then I deleted it, I promise. I kept the real one, the big one, the one that makes me sick. I began to even, dare I say, see my author-self take shape on the page. Caught a glimpse of what might be my own story, interspersed between the others'.

This is what is right. Right? If stories are a real thing then so are their characters. I have to decide who to let live. They come to me with needs and desires, like pets. Once I release them, they are not mine anymore. If I am to publish Pauline's truth, it is not a case of one sister creeping into another sister's bedroom and reading her notes. My story will fill in the blanks in Pauline's, will cast a dark light over her carefree adventures. She built a safe place to live, with a different Baby, without any trace of who he relentlessly reminded her he was in real life, over and over. And I have written him down, the real one, and placed him inside of her world. I have scribbled all over her words.

It has not been long, yet I can't help but feel that I am never in touch with Baby unless we are working. I've requested he help me, as some sort of olive branch. The nurse handles most things, then I get him when he is lucid. It must be all of the thinking. I've thought through whole decades, lying still under the covers in Catherine's room. When I come outside again, it is as if in spring.

The more I achieve distance through thought the more I feel like a stranger in the house. It is not that I have moved out in any official way, but I leave my things by the door, I announce where I am going when I leave the room, I'm careful with what I take from the refrigerator.

Today, he answers the door and is alive.

"I have it," he says.

He hurries me in, where he's set us up at the kitchen table, or the nurse did before he left. To one side, a tea towel folded in half and on top of it are two spoons, two mugs, a sugar bowl. This is the work of the nurse, to be sure.

I pour two mugs from the Thermos of coffee, stir cream into both, ignore the sugar.

"Well," I say. I take a sip. It's good. Good-bad. Familiar and unsophisticated. "Let's hear it."

"*A Fantastic Betrayal of My Character*," he says. With the phrase, he fans his hands out before him, as if presenting the title. At times he is so like a child that I cannot blame him for a thing. I consider he is perhaps not evil, but stupid—malformed.

"*A Fantastic Betrayal of My Character*," says Baby. "The final work."

"Okay," I say. "A Fantastic Betrayal of My Character." Somehow, psychically, he has stolen my "A." I feel silly for even entertaining the idea.

"And it begins, ah, how shall it begin."

"Well," I say. "It's pretty much finished. I've mostly finished the book by now."

He interrupts. "I have no blood left in the world. Something like that, no? I am the last of a chain of errors."

Has he forgotten which of his daughters is here?

There is a double frame on the kitchen island with two family photos, taken moments apart. I see it—am aware of it—each time I am in the kitchen, though I have not thought of it since childhood. Have not really looked. We, the four of us, are standing in front of Baby's previous Jeep, or maybe two ago. Our parents bookend us, me and Pauline. I am wearing overalls and a white T-shirt. I do not know how old I am, though I am pubescent.

There is something in my shape, in the way my clothes fit. It is as if the veil of sexlessness has been lifted. I am, at least in this moment captured, a regular person. And in my regularity, my neutral womanhood, there is sexuality. I appear soft and affected. A person I have never seen before. It's just, I've always seen photographs through my father's eyes. There has always been a staleness to me, in print.

"My ex-communication from the Arthurs!" says Baby, bringing me back. "A career of searching for myself. Searching and finding nothing!"

Maybe I am not his, either. Maybe I just never found the documentation. But, I see it in the lines on his face, in the way his hands are postured one on top of the other on the counter. I am made of his body.

I consider that now would be a good time to tell him about everything I've found through the DNA site. It startles me when Baby appears to be all here. Makes me wonder where he is hiding other times. And if he can come back, then is anything ever really lost? This both helps and hinders my ability to handle him. For, I don't often worry that I have lost him, and, when I have lost him, it will take me time to realize. The confirmation of his leave, never to return, will not come until death. Until then I will be waiting for another glimpse of lucidity.

"I sent invitations to some people from the DNA site," I say. I don't know why I tell him. Really I'm just getting his hopes up.

"How does it begin? Let's begin, 'just as a seed contains all of the potential to become a mighty tree, I was born with the makeup of destruction.'" He smiles. I am at the computer. He is angled outward, speaking to as much of the room as possible.

"And moreover, properly germinated by experts of chaos!"

"Are we starting over from scratch?" In front of me are hundreds of pages of work. Already I feel it leaving me. He will obliterate what is there, replace it, deny I ever wrote a word. But, he cannot take the words I write on my own.

"Write something about grandchildren. Address the book to my impossible grandchildren. I had something about that. A poem. Remember?"

"I don't," I say. "Sorry."

He is grasping at the table, searching for a pen and paper, or anything. He is alive with ideas, and no way to get them down.

His impossible grandchildren.

I am not too old to have children. I had the desire when it was novel. In my early twenties, it seemed an option. To be in the city, a young mother, always single when I imagined it, pushing a stroller down Queen Street, stopping in for coffee at some boutique café. It all makes me laugh. I feel I'm looking up at the underside of my life and my self. Were I to become a mother now, with my routines at Baby's house, with my non-relationship with Catherine, with my own mother so far away, with Pauline even further. I guess I'd always imagined motherhood with a certain relevance. The proximity of other mothers, the closure of ending myself in a way, beginning something else. But the women I already have in my life are infrequent, have little room

for me. It's not that I think I am a victim of withholding.
I understand I never learned to let them in.

So, were I to have a child, it would be one more perspective of disappointment cast over me and my behaviours
and my lacking qualities. We might have something for a
length of time. A precious secret something, a love without conditions. But then she—she—would grow, leave,
look back and say, "How could you have?" Because I know
I could not do it right. It was done wrong to me, and I
never put the time into learning otherwise. Professionals
speak in a code I do not like to navigate. I go into those
cold grey offices and whisper secrets and at the end of an
hour I am not what I am but a percentage of a shade off
of what I and all others should be. Fix the deviation. Oh,
it mends so heartlessly. To be numb and without edge, to
be vibrant and beloved. My exposure may have done me
in too early for there to be a reasonable chance of rerout-
ing. Again, I'm romanticizing my hurt. Most children are
kept in boxes. I saw in others in childhood that things
were hidden, other things simplified. There was a general
safety and comfort structured around them that allowed
them to relax into engagement with whatever was placed
before them. In school they were simply in school; they
looked forward to small things; they calmed when pla-
cated. I felt a weight on my body when I tried to sit still.
I developed an impending feeling of dread that was too
big for me to process, and my inability to grasp it was a
sign to me that something bad was coming. I bided my
time, waiting for the day I would grow into the horror of
losing context.

Baby took me for drives, sometimes to pick up the cases of wine he would get mixed at the big place outside the city, other times to have coffee and doughnuts in a parking lot on the east end, sometimes just to drive and then return home. On these drives he would explain to me the ways of the world. I don't remember when it began, but I know that it was before I was old enough to legally sit in the front seat. I remember getting out of the back when we parked, moving to the passenger seat.

One time in particular, when I was so small in the big leather passenger seat, he said, as if an aside, while peeling back the mouthpiece of a plastic coffee lid, "You know there's no God by now." I didn't know it either way. I was eating a vanilla doughnut, with small round colourful sprinkles falling into the cracks of the seat, sliding them out with my fingertip between my bare legs. It was summer, my skin was gluing itself to the leather with sweat, and there was a certain satisfaction in ripping them off, the burn afterwards. "Death is empty," he said, "just like life." I must have protested. I don't remember what I did, other than the small measured bites, trying to finish the childish treat, to join the world of adults. He said, oh, I don't remember, but something like: to outlive your art is to be a failure, but if your art outlives you, you will never know.

In other ways he exposed me to new things. We went to galleries, looked at gory paintings of religious sacrifice, watched young graduate students cut their skin on stages in rented hole-in-the-wall venues downtown. We went to jazz clubs and sat up front; sometimes I waved to the musicians, not yet having learned the largeness of the world, and developed an incessant buzzing in one ear from sitting a foot away from big box speakers. I hear it now. Just like my mother. I saw literary readings devolve into whole rooms shouting, I saw noise poetry consisting of a man screeching into a microphone until he passed out, I saw writers shake hands with writers in a game of sex and money. All of it, glamorous, all of it, pathetic.

If I cannot straighten myself out I at least can make an act out of my refusal to do what was done to me. And well nothing was done to me, or I don't remember anything ever having been done to me. When I think this to myself—nothing happened to me—my shoulders relax. So I will not reproduce. There are other, less complicated ways to be. There is a perfection in the unmade plan. Plus, I cannot lie—I enjoy the defiance of not giving Baby what he wants.

There is silence in the kitchen.

"Hillary would remember the poem, can you call her?"

I am trying to discern from the way he is looking at me who he thinks I am. Perhaps nobody. It is possible he is seeing me as who I truly am, right before his eyes, but that I am not "Hillary."

"Why don't you ever come to visit me?" He is joking, there are crinkles around the corners of his eyes. "Too busy for your old dad?"

It's Pauline. He thinks I'm Pauline. I feel like I am watching an old tape, or like I am dreaming. I back away the same as when I found the bug in her clothing.

"Men are dead ends," he says. "Write that! We need women."

Still, he is not back. He is gone behind his eyes.

FOR HALF OF THE car ride I am Pauline to him. Then silence.

If I were in one of my moods when I feel I can close myself off to emotion in favour of the work—the *work*, the great and holy *work*—I might pull over and write some of it down, what he was saying. If I hadn't washed Pauline completely out of the manuscript I might consider a situation such as this one a suitable scene.

By the time we pull into the parking lot behind the clinic I've more or less forgotten anything romantic or literary enough to be transcribed. That must be how things are for people like him all of the time: nothing is worth forgetting. Yes, of course I see the humour in the thought now, sitting next to him as he looks dumbly at the windshield. Not *through* it but *at* it. I really have learned to tell the difference.

The doctor wastes no time and, speaking only to me, explains that the lucid periods will eventually start to come on less frequently. Whereas before Baby would go and come back, he will begin not to come all the way back. Now, or not long from now. I don't know what's worse: the realization that I am losing my father, for real this time, or the realization that I wish only for him to come back one more time, just for the ceremony. I have become sick with my fixation on my work, just like him. A selfish part of me wants nothing to get in the way of the public celebration of the writing.

I am saddened by the way Baby does what the doctor tells him, and seems happy to do so. It seems a cruel thing to make him sit up on the medical bench, his feet swinging like a child.

"You're very lucky to have your daughter at home with you," the doctor says loudly at him.

"I'm sure he's sick of me," I say, and feel frustrated with the whole exchange.

I want to ask the doctor if there is some sort of pill, some sort of special routine, some exotic imported fruit the nectar of which brings clarity to the ailing mind. Instead I strain to see what he types into my father's file. I am unsuccessful.

The doctor is young, with a positive outlook that reminds me of our irrelevance to him at all times when we are not in his office. Baby's lucidity is not something he feels anxiety about. He is not considering methods of ensuring that we make it to the literary award ceremony in three days. In any case, if only I can convince the doctor things are dire enough, surely he will offer some sort of solution.

Baby clears his throat, swinging his legs with abandon.

"Osman," he says.

That's the doctor's name.

Dr. Osman turns in his swivel chair.

"A man walks into a psychiatrist's office. He's wearing pants made of cling wrap."

The doctor and I exchange a look.

"The psychiatrist says, 'Sir, I can clearly see your nuts.'"

Baby looks at the space between myself and the doctor. Then, we all laugh.

If only he'd act a bit more gone.

I am reminded of when my mother once took me to the doctor in childhood. I'd had this horrible cough, for weeks, but when we got into the doctor's office I didn't cough once. My mother pulled me out of there, fuming, saying I'd made a fool out of her for having brought me in with "nothing wrong." As if something was only wrong if somebody else said it was.

The doctor is pleased with Baby's current state and assures me that there is some time left.

A FANTASTIC BETRAYAL
OF MY CHARACTER
By Baby Davidson

Chapter I

The extravagant promotional event does not a writer make.

It is the eventual resignation to the *process*, the admission that all of the pleasure of the craft lies in anticipation. The unfinished manuscript, the sudden idea, the wait for the response from the agent or publisher. The writer works and waits. Whomever arrives at the event, tailored, groomed, cocktail in hand—that's someone else. The occasional and brief venture into fraternization always sends a writer scurrying back under the rock from whence they came. A colleague once said, "The relationship between the agent and the writer thrives in darkness." That is, communication is sparse.

Alas, the deals do get done. I was flown to New York and put up in a Manhattan hotel. I'd invited along two of my students, hoping to offer some sort of taste of *The Business*. There'd been a sudden sting of regret when we got buckled into the plane, realizing we'd not had a thing to talk about. I'd feigned sleep, then really did fall asleep, and when I awoke the girls were nudging me. We were there: New York City!

Many of the individuals in attendance I'd only before seen in photographs, in magazines and on the backs and inside covers of books. To have their eyes fixed on me, to shake their hands and not have had to tell them my name, it was surreal. Though it at first thrilled me, and I floated between groups of writers, editors, agents, feeling as if the night were representative of some sort of major shift in my trajectory, I quickly became overwhelmed.

It was during the fourth retelling of the process of writing the book—frenzied, without sleep, all through the nights to capitalize on the only quiet in my household, then, waking and showering, shaving, and dressing for work at the university— that I'd become suddenly uninterested in the whole ordeal.

"That's what it takes, eh," an older, unsuccessful writer, had said.

"No," I'd told him. "It's just how I do it."

I'd snuck outside to a phone booth and closed myself in, desiring a brief intermission. It would seem natural now for me to have phoned home. I do believe I'd wanted to. I'd wanted to hear their voices, my daughters. My wife's too, but I'd found myself wishing she could've said different things than I knew she'd have said, had I called.

When I re-entered, the girls had established themselves as popular figures in the room. A rush of envy, seeing them sur-rounded by men who were hungry and wolfish in posture, was replaced with a feeling of pride. They were wise beyond their years, I felt. I was lucky to have such students, lucky to shepherd them into the limelight. One day, perhaps they would become quite remarkable.

My agent, too, had his own business to do, his own hands to shake. This night belonged to everyone; my name on the sign outside was irrelevant.

I was suddenly overcome with a feeling of sadness, watching the girls. They had a certain ease of posture, a confident wide-mouthed laugh. I missed my family. I felt horror at the thought of my daughters in a room like that one, talking to men like those.

Had I approached the girls to warn them of my departure, to offer to bring them back with me, I worried I'd cut something short, something valuable and life-changing. I left them be, though not without worry that they might be rushed out by another man, pushed into a cab, and used up. I'd let the natural order of the world dictate the rest of the night, for them. For me, I could not withstand the remainder.

I made my way to the airport with increasing but happy impatience. Soon I would be in my house, under the bed linens beside my wife, my children long asleep. In the morning my having returned would be a surprise. The flight seemed to pass in an instant. I boarded, buckled my seatbelt, had a passing thought or two, and then I was retrieving my car from the airport parking lot, driving in the soft pink glow of the first hours of the day. I'd lost my handle on time. I'd figured somehow I would arrive home at the same hour as I'd left the literary event. Then, coming up the driveway with the weight of the weekend on my back, my head cutting through the fine mist of the morning, bringing a sting to my eyes, through which I saw the fogged-up kitchen window, four small handprints against the glass, and two small faces, alight with anticipation.

18

I'VE SENT OUT INVITATIONS to everyone I could think of, received a handful of sorry-nos. Though he is hounded by fans, industry professionals, and so on, I was hard-pressed to think of his friends. It surprised me when Baby asked me to reach out to my mother a second time, to insist, though didn't surprise me when she dismissed the idea. Catherine has arranged for flowers to be presented to Baby upon his arrival, by one of the members of the Arthurs, in case she herself can't make it. She is scheduled to have five dogs, can't seem to find a replacement. I feel on edge waiting for her confirmation, and try to expect a no. Especially after inviting the family members from the DNA site and having both of them, in other words, reply, "Who?"

Baby has asked me to speak—"be funny"—when he receives the award. I have prepared notes but not rehearsed them. My anticipation of spending time with Catherine is making me shaky. It's just I don't know how to *be* around her anymore. Am I allowed to stand close, to treat our

bodies as extensions of each other? Or is she an old friend
of my father, as he has always said? See, I'd hate for a new
distance to come out of my inaction.

Baby is going through his closet, asking me, "And whose
is this?" about a number of his suit jackets. On one end of
the rack is the yellow suit that he wore to see Pauline, life-
less on its hanger.

"Okay," I say, "and what about when they call your
name?"

He strokes the arm of a wine-coloured shirt. "Thank
you very much for this great and unexpected honour,"
he says.

I nearly scold him when I realize he is joking with me.

Something I have not considered: How would Pauline
have been had I been the one to go? I say "the one" as if it
had been a matter of chance—50/50 odds, in my favour.

"That one is yours," I say about a grey checked jacket.

Would Pauline have moved in too, I wonder? Would
they have eased back into the routines of her childhood?
He couldn't. Would he? Would she have done it anyway,
in the end? She was so troubled by large things. She fixated on death. She once told me, "I feel like a magnet
being pulled toward my end." She slept whenever possible, drank to keep herself out of the house, came home
and broke things, acted violently against anyone trying to
placate her. The big things, I understood. In fact, I asso-
ciated her acts of aggression with beauty. I see Pauline
behind every beautiful blonde. But the small nuanced danger of the household was lost on me. I saw the family as
heroic, something to aspire to. I wanted attention. I even

wanted . . . I can't say. Pauline knew I did, too. She saw me as small and neurotic, unable to understand a thing. She became frustrated by my inability to just be. These were the things I used to believe about myself and Pauline. These were our differences. However, the further I get from her the more certain I become that I did not understand at all. All along I knew that one of us had to be wrong, and I never expected that it could be me. For, it turns out, I was luckier than I could ever have known. Protected by the blood running under my skin.

I could have saved her if I had known. It would have saved me too. I know I shouldn't compare. Here I am. Saved? I live in aftermath and I measure time in the negative. Lately, some days, Baby seems not to remember Pauline at all. Sometimes I don't either. Other times he sees her where she isn't. For a moment the other day, I thought of my mother, and I thought of her in a way that I think of Pauline, by which I mean I know that I was operating as if she were dead. I sat with the thought for a moment before I remembered, oh! Despite the return to having my ideas straight, it proved impossible for me to understand that my mother was in the world, doing something, thinking something, at that very moment. In hypothetical, yes. But just as when I try to imagine the vastness that is beyond Earth, the vastness that is beyond the walls of the house when I am inside with the curtains closed, it simply did not seem to be real. Then, the same exercise with Catherine. Closer, plus I've seen the inside of her home. It is easy for me to imagine her doing things I have seen her do; she may be at the table eating lunch, she may be on the couch reading, she may be in the basement with one of the dogs. But something else, something perfectly believable such as organizing her dresser, washing her face. There seems to be no way. And in this way I feel stunned by the sudden realization that I do not believe there is a world outside of my experience. That I do not believe, were I to go to where Pauline is, that things would continue on. And this makes me wonder if this was Pauline's way of finally having control. Locking us into our patterns, ensuring that we live out the rest of our lives in a circuit, picking up pieces that were once together.

Unsurprisingly Baby has decided to wear the yellow suit. I brought it upon myself. When he asked, "Whose is this?" and pulled the yellow sleeve out from the body, I said nothing as I was lost in thought. This caused him to take special notice. Perhaps he preferred it, imagining it belonged to somebody else. Being somebody else was a special passion of Baby's. He is wearing the jacket over top of a slack grey T-shirt, sweatpants.

There is a possibility that he is wearing the suit out of spite. Yes, that must be it, even if he doesn't know it. Some friction against Pauline. All along, he has hated her. Surely that is why I was spared. Never have I been more relieved by his disdain. For, there must not have been as much per-version as there was punishment. Oh, how I can disturb myself right out of my skin.

I am running out of time to get ready for this evening. My hair is wild and unwashed, but to wash and style it would use up all of what I have. I will have to settle for makeup and something taken from one of the other women in my family. I leave Baby to fend for himself in the closet, go to look through my boxes from Pauline. On my way to the ceremony I will wear my mother's mink coat over top of whatever I borrow from Pauline.

Pauline's formal wear is in the other box I picked up from the roommate, the one that I have left sealed. The other I have brought in from the garage, picked through, worn or at least tried on some things. With a ballpoint pen I scrape through the brown packaging tape, worry I may be drawing a straight blue line across some folded garment. When I pry open the box flaps the top layer is small bunches of pink, beige, and white lace. Thongs, crotchless panties, wireless bras. I arrange them on my bedspread and as I'm laying out a white G-string I see that many of the pieces are unwashed.

There is a feeling in my body that for a moment I sit with, still and silently. I wait to hear evidence of Baby being consumed by some task, though he would never come through a closed door, anymore. He seems to not want to see anything he is unprepared for. The regular information of the day already overwhelms him.

I imagine the roommate, or maybe even the roommate's family, or a police officer or hired cleaner taking Pauline's lingerie, maybe her laundry, and putting it in a box. Touching each piece, folding them. I lie down on the bed next to the rows of panties, lying in such a way so that my face rests on the white soiled G-string, not touching it with my hands, relieving myself of intention, acting with two minds, one of them playing out a lie. And I smell Pauline and I am with Pauline, and later when I arrive at the ceremony with the lace under my clothes I will be Pauline, too.

What if these bugs really are the same bugs that fed on Pauline? What if for Pauline it all came down to the infestation? Suddenly I fear, if that is so, that it might happen to me too. I mean I've already lost Pauline. What more can be expected of me in a calendar year? To wash, to inspect, to exterminate, to exterminate again. It really could do me in. But I am belittling Pauline. It's just I'd prefer it be the bugs than anything else, considering the other things. There is a simple romance to this having been her breaking point. A beautiful woman in a two-bedroom apartment, draped in silk, covered in insect bites, over-wrought. Another example of my not having a penchant for the written word. Then, a thought. Pauline's bugs surviving in the box of lingerie means Pauline's blood is inside of the bugs in the box. My blood and Pauline's blood in the bugs in the lingerie that I am wearing at the literary ceremony in the church on Bloor Street. Well, I know it is not the same blood. Generations of bugs must have lived in the apartment. Feeding on her roommate in the night. Their heritage in part being Pauline. Their meals, their rituals. Perhaps even religious ceremonies around feeding on Pauline. Their parents' parents' bodies replenished and rebuilt out of Pauline.

I squeeze one of the bites hard and clear fluid forms a small perfect sphere on top of my skin. Then the pain stops me from continuing. I can't bring myself to throw out the G-string; besides, the other garments are on my bedspread. I must instead accept the infestation. In bed with the lingerie, I feel I am the same sexual girl from the photograph in the kitchen. Someone I perhaps would have been, always, otherwise.

BECAUSE OF THE WAY the road loops around the lake, the longer way goes past the exit we'd take for the train station, if we were picking up my mother. She has given a final answer: no. Though she has had second thoughts about Christmas; I am once again invited. Just me, that is. Baby is consumed by himself anyway, and so won't challenge the right turn out of the driveway in lieu of the faster left. He smells of aftershave, the nurse having done a clean job. I even invited him to come, the nurse, forgetting he was simply at work.

Catherine outside playing tug-of-war with a handful of dogs. She's cleared off most of the front yard now, a task I appreciate due to my inability to carry it out in any proper way. She is wearing a long coat that looks like a quilt, pyjama pants, and rain boots, and she's leaping, dancing each time she yanks at the piece of rope. I am ashamed to be taking great solace in the image of her in her yard. As if my enjoyment, unknown to her, is a perversion.

Baby rolls down his window and smacks the hood of the car with his mitten in this old familiar way. I am reminded of their closeness, and the newness of my closeness with Catherine. There is something between them that is greater than I am. She looks up, waves, hurries inside. So she has sorted out care for the dogs.

It is for the best that my mother is not here with us. Then Catherine might change her mind.

"What shall I say the book is called?" says Baby. "The title is no good, I can't use the one we have."

"You changed your mind?"

"It's no good."

"Well." I can see through a window Catherine is hurrying from room to room. The dogs must be going wild at her feet. "What else, then?"

"Something from the Bible," says Baby.

"Okay," I say.

"To Know Not What We Do."

"Too wordy, I think."

"The New Is Here."

"No good," I say.

"To Be Like Wool," he says. "Delight to Show Mercy."

"I don't know."

"I'll think of it when we get there," he says. "Be funny when you introduce me. I'll think of it while they're laughing."

"Why don't I just think of it?" I say. "Since, you know."

"It's my life's work," he says. "Hillary, it's very important."

"Yes, I know, Dad." I can feel sweat on my face, and worry my makeup will be ruined. "I wrote it."

In the doorway of the house, a man perhaps a few years younger than me. Slim, tall, wheat-coloured hair. I've entirely forgotten she has a son, erased him. He smiles at our vehicle, looks straight through the windshield into my eyes, or so it feels. Then, Catherine is ready, just like that, and joins us.

"My goodness," she says to me. "Hillary, you look," and she stops, and I turn and smile out the window.

WE ENTER AS A FORCE. I feel something strange standing between Catherine and Baby, something familial. But, I feel too the guilt of my mother.

My head is swimming. Everyone is here; the Arthurs, Mark Richman, some people from the publishing company, Pauline, Baby, Catherine, various people in the industry whom I've seen or seen photos of. I said Pauline. Of course she isn't. Otherwise, the turnout is nothing too big, not too many non-industry attendees. People pass us, some smile in a way they're smiling at everyone else. A man or two stop Baby, say something along the lines of, "You're still here?" Obviously I exaggerate.

When I see Catherine from various areas of the room I am struck by her posture, by the way she holds her face. Her hair, her frame, are so beautiful. You wouldn't believe it. I can hardly believe she is one of us. Well, in a way. The way any of us are.

Baby looks smaller than he ever has to me. His mouth is a thin line with the weight of his whole face holding it closed. He hunches, scuttles from table to table, I figure looking for copies of his work. Despite the size of his name on the event poster projected onto the stage, there are few people for him to speak with. It is all shaping up to be a bit of a punch in the gut.

I think of the family members found through the DNA site, and the event feels small. The contacts from the

DNA site dismissing my invitation recontextualizes Baby and his world, for me. I've always assumed a largeness about literature. As if all lives are shaped around it just like my own. But other people have other things; they watch movies, they follow touring bands on the road.

Slowly the Arthurs begin to gather in a half-circle, observing the room together. Baby joins, and I worry he will be ridiculed, but he is welcomed. Something about those men, together, feels natural. They are boisterous, patting each other on the back, nodding and grinning. I am able to relax for the first time since entering. It isn't just him. They are all hunched, grey.

The passage of time is punctuated with small plastic cups of wine.

My body feels electric when I watch Catherine move through the room, searching for me, I suppose. I catch her eye, grin at her, and slip out of the main hall and into the bathroom. There is a tall skinny mirror mounted to a part of the wall set back farther than the rest. This gives me a feeling of being boxed in. The blouse I have buttoned over Pauline's bra is cut low, exposing pink lace. Under my skirt I can feel the soft silk of the panties. I make no expression at the mirror. Back myself into a stall and lock it with both locks. Somebody else enters the bathroom and sets down a number of small objects on the counter, hovers by the mirror. I can see the scaly pointed toes of snakeskin boots.

When I pull up my skirt, pull down my pantyhose, there are pink welts on my thighs and on my kneecaps. I make an X with my nail in one of the larger oblong-shaped spots on my left thigh, feel the familiar sick pain of the allergy to insect venom. In a panic, I strip the pantyhose down off my legs, stay seated on the toilet and lift my feet to slip the underwear over the white patent boots I've gotten from another box of Pauline's.

I return to the audience as they are inviting the Arthurs up onto the stage.

The men on stage are proud, stiff in formal dress, moving in awkward formation with a long-absent fifth. I walk in such a way so that I can apply some friction to some of the itching areas on my inner thighs. When I clench my left knee as my right leg takes a step I can affect one of the lower bites. I feel myself crawling though I must be imagining it. I think of Gregor Samsa, resist a smirk across my face.

In the schedule I was given at the door there is a biography of Baby, a list of publications, and a brief blurb on his forthcoming work: *Baby Davidson's forthcoming memoir chronicles a man entering complete and total isolation. The story is one of resignation, of suicide of personhood, and experimentation with greed, absence, and observation. An experience of death in life.* These are Mark Richman's words. *The Death of My Name* is Baby Davidson's self-proclaimed "final work."

I am caught up in the pamphlet when it is announced that Baby has won the "Most Influential Ontario Writer" award. The man doing the talking, one of the Arthurs I recognize from younger photographs but whose name I do not know, announces that they would like to formally invite Baby back in. I wonder if this is a challenge.

The group of them up there, all old and dressed in wool, and bespectacled and leaning on one another, remind me so much of Baby I feel a hopelessness of identity. In any case, this announcement is my cue. I enter the stage. Eyes are visible but not enough to identify.

I pause for a moment and take in the room. *Be funny*, I remember.

"When I was growing up," I say. "I asked my dad, 'What's the difference between the kind of doctor you are and the kind who helps sick people?' And he said, 'Well, I don't have any patience.'"

There are a few laughs.

Catherine is smiling. Baby is clapping his hands, looks elated. When he asked me to present him the honour I felt in a small way that he was bringing me into his world, and that this might mean I am becoming more of what he is. But I am only ever what he tells me. My story is only the most recent he's written. He told me first to be a daughter, then to be—in a way—a partner, then to be a nurse, now to be . . .

There is applause. Soon it will quiet. I will exit the stage, exit the building. I will wait behind the steering wheel the amount of time it takes for my drunkenness to fade, for my vision to stabilize. Then I will drive home, wherever that is now, go upstairs and slip into bed. I will wake tomorrow and begin my work on being something good. Something of my own. Maybe if I am so good I will not even be me anymore. I will be so good that I drive others crazy, and I will have my perfect routines, and I will find something bigger than anything here on the ground, and I will dry up all of my juicy perversions and be empty, without any eggs left for any of the men in Orillia, and I will lie in my sheets and let the bugs feast on their good, God-sent meal. And when they have eaten me up I will be with Pauline, both of us inside of the bugs, together.

Baby replaces me on stage. He thanks the crowd, the Arthurs, Mark Richman. There is a new work coming, he says, called *The Death of My Name*.

"It is a memoir," says Baby. "Written by my daughter, Hillary."

Catherine elbows me, as if something light has just happened, a joke. People in the audience, those who recognize me, turn and look. If it was a mistake, a lapse, if it will be taken back in the morning, still in this moment we finally live in truth.

How strange it is that such a thing can happen so quickly, so quietly, and by accident. That a lightness can overtake me almost without warning, can threaten to lift me out of the room entirely.

And though he has just ended himself up there, I find I cannot imagine that Baby won't live forever, somehow.

He has just ended his career, will sink back into the anonymous body of Marcus Greene, and it occurs to me that I do not know who that is, or who he will be, and I wonder if he has enough time left for me to find out.

In a way, in a sort of ugly way, the family is all together. I am drunk. I am with my father, his colleagues, Catherine. Everyone fits together in a way in which I feel I am able to step away, let things be. Tomorrow I will begin work on something of my own.

ACKNOWLEDGEMENTS

Thank you to my family: Mom, Dad, and Aunt Beth, and to my good friends: Elliot Burns, Ali Pinkney, André Babyn, Jake Morrow, Joshua Chris Bouchard, Sophie McCreesh, Khashayar Mohammadi, Mary Germaine, Cody Caetano, Zak Jones, Joseph MacNeil, Jack Christie, and Quinn Mason.

Thank you to Professor Robert McGill and the University of Toronto Graduate English Department, to my outstanding agent Stephanie Sinclair at CookeMcDermid, to Harriet Alida Lye for the invaluable editorial guidance, and to brilliant editor Kelly Joseph and everyone at M&S.

Thank you always to the Canada Council for the Arts for the ongoing support.

FAWN PARKER is the author of the novels *Set-Point* and *Dumb-Show* and the forthcoming poetry collection *Jolie Laide*. She is co-founder of BAD NUDES MAGAZINE and BAD BOOKS PRESS, and president at The Parker Agency. Her story, "Feed Machine," was longlisted for the 2020 Writers' Trust McClelland & Stewart Journey Prize. Parker lives between Toronto, Ontario, and Fredericton, New Brunswick.